In memory of my grandfather,
William Edmund Conroy

—A. C.

A Peachtree Junior Publication

Published by
PEACHTREE PUBLISHERS
1700 Chattahoochee Avenue
Atlanta, Georgia 30318-2112

www.peachtree-online.com

Text © 2005 by Anne Capeci
Illustrations © 2005 by Paul Casale

Book design by Melanie McMahon Ives

Photographs from the author's family collection; illustrations by Paul Casale.

Manufactured in China
10 9 8 7 6 5 4 3 2 1
First Edition

Library of Congress Cataloging-in-Publication Data

Capeci, Anne.
   Missing! / written by Anne Capeci ; illustrated by Paul Casale.-- 1st ed.
      p. cm. -- (The Cascade Mountain railroad mysteries ; no. 4)
   Summary: During the 1920s, as Billy, Finn, and Dannie investigate a series of thefts in a
railroad workers camp, they also find themselves searching for Billy's missing cousin, nine-
year-old Mim.
   ISBN 1-56145-334-X
   [1. Missing persons--Fiction. 2. Robbers and outlaws--Fiction. 3. Cousins--Fiction. 4.
Sex role--Fiction. 5. Railroads--Fiction. 6. Northwest, Pacific--History--20th century--
Fiction. 7. Mystery and detective stories.] I. Casale, Paul, ill. II. Title.

PZ7.C17363Mi 2005
[Fic]--dc22

                                2004019475

CASCADE MOUNTAIN
4
RAILROAD MYSTERIES

MISSING!

ANNE CAPECI

Ω
PEACHTREE
ATLANTA

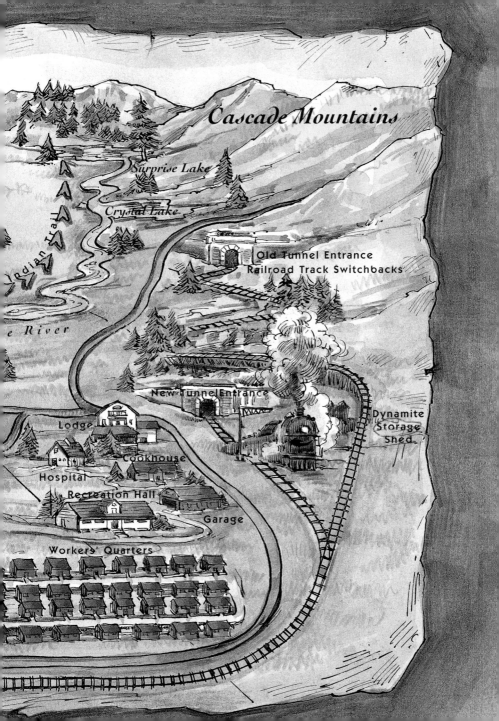

Acknowledgments

The author would like to thank the following people for their invaluable help in researching and preparing this book: David Conroy, Margaret Conroy Capeci, and Elizabeth (Buffy) Rempel for the wonderful stories and memories that made this series possible; Pete Conroy, for generously allowing the use of his photographs; Eva Anderson, author of *Rails Across the Cascades,* which provided wonderful historical information; Lisa Banim, for her expert guidance in helping to shape the story; and the Great Northern Railway Historical Society, for helping me to find detailed information about how the Cascade Tunnel was built.

Table of Contents

Chapter One
GOOD-BYE AND HELLO

Scenic, Washington
1926

Billy Cole stepped to the edge of the train platform.
The boxlike cars of the Northern Express stretched
along the tracks like beads on a string. Steam from the
engine swirled around the cars. It took some of the
chill off the sharp wind that blew down the Cascade
Mountains toward the Scenic work camp.

Billy only faintly heard the drills and pumps and
diesel engines that pounded away inside the new railroad tunnel.

Winter is coming, he thought. *No doubt about it.*

The leaves of the vine maple and alder had already
turned. They made splashes of red among the green fir
trees that covered the Cascades. In just a few moments,

the Northern Express would chug past those trees on its way east over the mountains.

And it would be taking Billy's friend Philip Mackey with it.

"I sure wish you could stay for the Fall Fish Fry," Billy said. He grinned up at Philip, who leaned out of the train.

"And for the first snowball fights," added Billy's good buddy, Finn Mackenzie.

Finn and Billy's other best pal, Dannie Renwick, had come to say good-bye to Philip, too. The three of them stood on the platform with their collars flipped up against the cold. Dannie's retriever Buster sniffed at the feet of the people who had come to see off Philip and his dad.

"Once the first storms hit, we'll build a snow fort to beat 'em all!" Dannie told Philip.

Philip leaned farther out the railcar window. His blond hair fell over his forehead, but it didn't hide the sadness in his eyes. "I wish I could stay, too. Father says Mr. Cole's doing such a fine job that we're not needed here."

Billy's chest swelled with pride. After all, Mr. Cole was his father. He was in charge of the work crews that were blasting the new tunnel through the mountains.

And here was Mr. Mackey, one of the biggest owners of the Great Northern Railway, praising his work!

"Father wants to get home to Chicago in time for Mother's birthday next week," Philip went on. "But you hook some trout for me, okay?"

"You bet I will," Billy told him. Sure, his old rod was nicked and battered. But there wasn't a boy in Scenic who was better at catching fish than Billy Cole. Or many men, either. "You remember your promise, too," he told Philip in a low voice.

"What's this about a promise?" asked Mr. Mackey, who had just finished shaking hands with Billy's father and the other adults on the platform. He gazed curiously at Philip as he stepped over to Billy, Finn, and Dannie.

"It's just something between us, Father," Philip said. "Don't worry, Billy. I won't forget."

To Billy's relief, Mr. Mackey didn't ask any more questions. He just clapped his hands briskly together and said, "Well! We'd better be on our way. We don't want to hold up the train."

Billy saw the engineer and brakeman inside the locomotive. They were gazing back through the mist at the crowd that had gathered. As soon as Mr. Mackey stepped onto the railcar, a loud whistle blasted. With a grinding of its wheels, the Northern Express chugged slowly forward.

"Bye, Philip!" called Billy, Dannie, and Finn.

Philip opened his mouth, but his words were drowned by a second piercing whistle blast. All he could do was wave while the train moved farther along the tracks. Billy, Finn, and Dannie waved and shouted back. They didn't stop until the Northern Express disappeared beneath one of the wooden sheds that protected the tracks from snow slides in the winter.

"Think he'll keep his promise?" Dannie asked.

Finn shrugged and stuffed his hands in the pockets of his knickers. "Sure. Why not?"

"He'll do it if he can," Billy agreed. "We'll just have to wait and see, I guess."

* * *

As the noise of the train faded away, Billy heard a new sound—the high, tinny beep of an automobile horn.

He turned toward the road that wound up the mountainside. Above Scenic, the gravel road turned into dirt tracks. Thick evergreens hid much of the road from view, but Billy saw a black sedan through the trees. Its tires kicked up dust and rocks as it sped toward Scenic. Billy grinned when he saw the curly red hair of the girl who waved from the backseat.

"It's Mim!" he shouted. "Mother! Dad! They're here!"

"Already?" Billy's mother shaded her eyes and gazed at the approaching automobile. "Why, so they are!" she said.

Billy was already racing down the depot steps to the road.

"Is that your cousin Mim?" Finn called after him.

Billy's Uncle Herb was helping to build the new tunnel, too. He and Aunt Delia and Mim lived in Berne, on the other side of the Cascade Mountains from Scenic. A camp town had sprung up there, just like the one in Scenic. While men in Scenic blasted through the mountains from the west, work crews in Berne dug from the east. Billy's father estimated it would be another year or longer before the two holes met deep inside the mountain.

That was fine with Billy. He loved living in Scenic while the tunnel was being built. And he was glad to have family close by. Sure, Mim was only nine, a full year younger than him. But they had always been great pals. And now Mim was coming to visit for a whole week while her parents went on to visit Mim's aunt.

As soon as Uncle Herb stopped his sedan, Mim burst from the backseat and ran over to Billy.

"I brought my marbles," she announced. "You'd better watch out, Billy. I've been practicing lots. I'll beat you for sure!"

"Patience, Miriam!" Aunt Delia scolded. She gave a good-natured shake of her head as she and Uncle Herb climbed from the front of the sedan. "You haven't even said hello yet."

Billy's father always said that Mim had more bounce than a rubber ball. That sure was true today. She hopped from foot to foot while Billy's parents exclaimed over how much she had grown. She barely stood still long enough to thank Billy's mother for the new red scarf she had knit for her. By the time Billy and his little sister Marjorie finished hugging Aunt Delia and Uncle Herb, Mim had already moved on to something new.

"I don't remember that dog." Mim ran toward the fir trees that grew alongside the road. Buster darted among the low branches, chasing pine squirrels. "He's a beauty!" Mim exclaimed.

"That's Buster," Dannie said proudly. "He's mine."

Mim smiled at Dannie. "I wish I could have a dog, but Dad won't let me," she said. "Dogs make him sneeze."

"Well, you can play with Buster while you're here, anyhow," Dannie said, her dark eyes shining with interest. Usually Dannie got on better with boys than girls. But Mim was as rough and tumble as any boy Billy knew. He could tell Dannie liked her already.

"These are my friends Dannie and Finn," Billy told Mim.

"Hey! Let's *all* play marbles," Mim suggested. "I have plenty to go around."

Billy smiled to himself. He was the one who had taught Mim to play marbles in the first place. That had been in the summer, the last time he'd visited Mim in Berne. Billy had missed shots on purpose so he wouldn't beat her too badly. He was sure he'd be doing the same thing today. But he wasn't about to tell Mim that.

"We won't play for keeps," he said. That meant Mim would get all her marbles back after the game, even if she lost.

"You don't have to go easy on me," Mim insisted. "I'm a crackerjack player now!"

Billy just nodded. Picking up a stick, he began to draw a large circle in the dirt next to the road. His parents and Aunt Delia and Uncle Herb were talking together on the porch of the old lodge. It had been a ski lodge before the railway took it over. Billy had heard his father mention those "crazy Swedes" from Seattle who had risked their necks on the steep slopes. Now Scenic's security office, telegraph room, post office, company store, and ticket office took up the first floor. Billy's father and the other managers had offices on the second floor. But everyone still called the building "the Lodge."

"We brought Mim's fishing tackle," Uncle Herb was saying. "She wouldn't miss the fish fry for anything."

"I might just take a few hours to hook some trout myself," said Mr. Cole.

Billy was surprised to hear that. His father never took time off work. Then again, folks in camp had been talking about the fish fry for weeks—and about the contest that would take place beforehand. There was a five-dollar prize for whoever caught the most fish.

His father went on talking to Aunt Delia and Uncle Herb. He was whispering now. There was some chuckling, and then Mr. Cole cleared his throat.

"Billy, would you run up to my office and bring our fishing gear down?" he said. "I brought it over from the cabin this morning."

Billy glanced up from the circle he had drawn. Mim was arranging her marbles in an X at the center of the ring. "We're just about to start," Billy objected. But then he said quickly, "Oh, all right." He didn't want to get in trouble the very first day of Mim's visit.

As he ran up the lodge steps, he felt his parents' eyes on him. They were smiling at him, and so were Aunt Delia and Uncle Herb, as if they knew something he didn't. Billy was glad to get inside, away from their stares.

Upstairs in his father's office he spotted his father's rod right away, leaning against the wall behind his cluttered desk. Next to it was a second fishing pole, one Billy had never seen before. A red ribbon was tied to the tip of the rod. A sign that read FOR BILLY dangled from the hook.

"Jeepers!" Billy breathed.

The rod was made of split bamboo, with a cork handle and a neat metal casting reel. It was so sleek, so perfect, that Billy hardly dared to touch it.

But at last he picked it up. After turning it over in his hands, he carried it carefully downstairs and out to the porch along with his father's rod and gear.

"It's mine?" he asked his parents. "For real?"

"I don't see any other Billy around here," Mr. Cole teased. He put an arm around Billy's shoulders. "Good luck today, son. I hope you win the prize."

"Thanks, Dad!"

Billy was dying to try out his new fishing pole. The sooner the better! But Finn and Dannie and Mim were waiting for him next to the marble ring. *The contest won't start for another few hours,* Billy reminded himself.

Very carefully he leaned his rod against the porch railing.

"Let's play marbles!" he said.

CHAPTER TWO

BEGINNER'S LUCK

Yippee! I did it again!" Mim cried.

She grinned as her shooter marble banged against Billy's and knocked it out of the ring. "You owe me two more marbles, Billy."

"Gee, Mim. You *have* been practicing," he said.

Billy looked down at the six marbles he'd won so far. Mim had five. Now he had to give her two as a penalty for having his shooter knocked from the ring. Billy tried not to mind.

"Here you go," he said, handing over the marbles. He blew on his hands to warm them up and his breath made a white cloud in the cold air.

Mim was knuckling down inside the ring, where her shooter had stopped. She tucked her scarf into her jacket so it wouldn't brush against the marbles. Then she curled her finger around her shooter, rested her knuckle against the ground, and used her thumb to flick the shooter across the ring. Billy frowned as a marble went scuttling outside the ring.

"One more and she wins the game," Finn said. He and Dannie had just two marbles each.

Mim looked carefully at the remaining marbles. A moment later she sent her shooter flying toward a cat's-eye.

Crack!

Her shooter banged into the marble.

"I did it!" Mim crowed as it rolled outside the ring. "I won!"

"Wow. You're good!" exclaimed Dannie.

Billy felt a bubble of jealousy rise up inside him. He had to bite his tongue to keep from saying that it was just beginner's luck. Or that she had only won because he'd gone easy on her. The truth was, he had played as hard as he knew how. Mim had won fair and square.

"I won! I won! I won!" Mim sang. The way she danced around the ring, waving her yellow shooter, only made Billy more annoyed.

"All right, Miss Big Shot," he said, rolling his eyes. "But I'm going to win the fishing contest."

"We'll see about that." Mim gave a sly smile as she

scooped her marbles into their bag. "I've gotten better at fishing, too, you know," she said.

"Well, I'm still going to win that five dollars," Billy bragged. "See if I don't!"

"I know! Why don't we have our own contest?" Dannie said. She grinned at Billy. "We'll see who can catch more fish, you and Finn, or Mim and me."

Billy looked over his shoulder at Finn. His friend nodded. "You're on!" Billy said. After all, no other kid had ever beat him at fishing.

Uncle Herb was placing Mim's suitcase and fishing gear on the lodge porch. "We'll be with Delia's sister and the new baby until next Saturday. You be good, Mim," he said.

There were hugs all around, and then Billy found himself waving good-bye for the second time that day.

"Well, I guess that's that," Billy's father said after Uncle Herb's sedan disappeared through the trees. He pulled his watch from his pocket. "What do you say we hike up now and get our pick of spots along the river?"

That was all Billy needed to hear. "Let's go!" he said.

In his mind, he pictured the exact bend in the Tye River where he wanted to fish. It was just below the falls that spilled out of Crystal Lake, about two miles up the mountain from Scenic. A flat rock jutted into the river at the bend. Billy had caught lots of fish there before. Big ones.

I'll show Mim who's the better fisherman, he thought.

"You'll need these," said Mrs. Cole. She set a basket of sandwiches down next to Mim's fishing gear. Folded on top was a bright red scarf she had knit for Billy when she knit the one for Mim. She'd stitched BILLY COLE in black letters next to the red fringe. Billy tied the scarf around his neck. Then he took his new fishing pole from where it leaned against the railing.

"Ready, Dad?" he asked.

Only then did he notice the man who had stopped on the lodge porch to talk to his father. He had dark hair and a stooped-over way of standing. Still, Billy saw the angry sparks in his eyes.

"Now see here, Mr. Cole," the man was saying. "You can't just go and take away a man's job for no reason."

"I had my reasons. You know that, Judd," Billy's father said calmly. He crossed his arms in front of his chest. "What you did put the lives of every man on your crew in danger—"

Mr. Cole suddenly stopped talking. He turned to Billy. "You kids go on ahead without me," he said gruffly. "I'll catch up later."

Billy wasn't about to argue. "Yes, sir," he said.

He started down the road toward the family cabins with his friends. Beyond the cabins a path led past the schoolhouse and up the mountain along the river. Billy tested the weight of his new rod as he walked along. It had just the right amount of give. The handle felt perfect in his palm.

"Look out, fish, here I come!" he crowed.

* * *

"How many do we have now, Billy?" Finn asked.

Billy reached over the side of the rock where he and Finn sat. All afternoon they had been fishing at Billy's favorite spot, just below Crystal Lake. The autumn chill had crept under his scarf and collar. Billy could hardly feel his hands anymore, but he didn't care.

He pulled a long line of speckled trout from the icy water next to the rock. "Eight, ten, twelve..." he mumbled as he counted the fish. "Sixteen in all!" he announced. "And I hooked ten of them!"

He cast out his line, then sat back to wait for his next bite.

"What about Mim and Dannie? How many do you think they have?" Finn asked.

Billy peered downstream. Up and down the river the

banks were crowded with men, women, and children. Billy had never seen so many people fishing. Laughing voices echoed through the trees. Billy spotted Mim and Dannie about twenty-five feet away, standing on the bank. He didn't see any fish. But he knew they could be strung on a line out of sight, just as his and Finn's were.

As Billy watched, the tip of Mim's rod gave a sharp tug downward. "Mim's just hooked one," he said. He frowned when he saw the plump trout she reeled in.

"Never mind about that," Finn told him. "Just wait 'til the girls see our catch. Sixteen trout! No one can top that!"

Billy nodded. The sun was sinking in the sky. The contest couldn't last much longer.

Sure enough, a few minutes later came the whistle blast that announced the end of the contest. Billy was just pulling his line of fish from the river when Mim and Dannie came running up.

"We've got eighteen trout!" Dannie said excitedly.

"And guess who caught eleven of them?" Mim added. Her cheeks were red and her eyes glowed with excitement. "Me!"

"Eleven?" Billy felt like a balloon with all the air let out of it. "You're sure?"

"Hey, that's one more than Billy!" Finn said before Billy could stop him. "We only caught sixteen between us."

Mim and Dannie whooped and jumped up and down together. "Ha! I guess you won't be winning that five dollars after all, Billy," Mim teased.

Billy couldn't bring himself to look at his younger cousin. He turned away—then groaned. Coming down the path from Crystal Lake were half a dozen boys and girls. It figured that Alice Ann Lockhart was at the front of the group. She was the biggest know-it-all in Billy's class at school. And she never missed a chance to pester Billy.

Dannie told Alice Ann about their contest.

"Gee, Billy, I guess you're just second best," Alice Ann said. "Even with that fancy new rod of yours."

Billy felt the sting of humiliation in his cheeks. *Don't let Alice Ann get to you,* he told himself.

But she *had* gotten to him. And so had Mim. How could she have won the contest? As he stood there, looking at the smug smiles on both girls' faces, Billy's anger bubbled over.

"You don't know anything!" he burst out.

Everyone stared at him, but Billy paid no mind. He shoved the line of trout into Finn's hands and grabbed his tackle box and his new rod. Then he stormed off into the woods.

"Hey! Come back!" Finn called. "Where are you going?"

Billy didn't know, and he didn't care. He walked blindly, barely looking at the fir trees and boulders he passed. The other kids' teasing laughter echoed inside his head. It pushed him deeper and deeper into the woods.

He wasn't sure how far he'd gone when at last he dropped down onto a granite boulder to rest.

"Second best, huh?" he muttered to himself.

He couldn't hear the river anymore. Or any people, either. Shadows were settling over the trees. The sun had already dipped behind the Cascades. The wind that whistled through the woods had grown sharper and colder. Billy's boots and jacket sleeves, wet from the river, felt like ice against his skin.

A shiver rippled through him. All at once the hairs on the back of Billy's neck stood on end. He had the strange feeling that someone was watching him.

Whirling around, he stared into the trees behind him. A black-tailed deer leaped over some rocks and disappeared behind a fir tree.

"So it was just you, eh, fella?" he murmured.

But the prickly feeling at the back of his neck didn't go away. Even after he'd started back toward camp, Billy kept looking behind him. It seemed like forever before he reached the old Indian trail along the river. It was deserted now.

Everyone must have gone back to camp, Billy realized.

He picked up his pace, fighting back the shivers that kept sneaking up on him. At last he saw the two-room schoolhouse at the very edge of camp. Its sloped roof was black against the evening sky. Farther on, through the trees, Billy saw the lights of the family cabins. It was a comforting sight. He ran toward them as fast as he could.

Mim was standing in the clearing at the center of the family cabins. Billy was so relieved to be home that he forgot to be mad at her.

"Mim!" he called out.

Billy's mother and father were there, too. In fact, just about everyone who lived in the family cabins was milling about.

They must be on their way to the recreation hall for the fish fry, Billy thought.

"Billy!" Mim broke away from the group and ran over to him. "Something awful has happened!"

Her eyes were wide and scared. Looking around, Billy

saw that his mother had her arm around Mrs. Lock-hart's shoulders. Mr. Cole stood among a group of men who were talking seriously. Everywhere Billy turned he saw frowning, worried faces.

"What is it?" he asked. "What happened?"

Dannie and Finn hurried up behind Mim. "Things were stolen from the cabins," Finn said. "There's a thief in camp!"

CHAPTER THREE

A THIEF IN SCENIC

A thief!" Billy exclaimed. "What got stolen?"

"Lots of stuff. They're still trying to figure it out," Dannie told him.

A thick knot of people stood around Alice Ann a few feet away. Her eyes were red. Her cheeks were wet and smudged where she had wiped away tears.

"He went right inside our cabin!" Alice Ann was saying. "Now Father's new coat is gone. Mother left an apple pie on the windowsill, and it's gone, too! Can you imagine?"

"I heard Mr. Riley say things are missing from his cabin also," Alice Ann's friend Lucy Grinnell spoke up. "A pair of binoculars. And ten dollars from his bill-fold."

"Ten dollars!" Billy whistled. That was a whole lot of money. "No one saw anything?"

Alice Ann shook her head. "How could we? Most folks were fishing, or getting the recreation hall ready for the fish fry," she said.

"Everyone but you, Billy," a voice spoke up.

Billy found himself looking into Wes Gundy's round face. Wes was the same age as Billy, but they didn't always get along.

"So where *did* you go after you stormed off on your own?" Wes asked. Billy didn't like the way Wes's eyes bored into him. Or the funny way everyone else was looking at him.

"You think *I* stole those things? You take that back!" Billy yelled.

Leaping forward, he grabbed Wes's collar. He would have knocked Wes to the ground, or tried to, if Finn, Mim, and Dannie hadn't dragged him back.

"Billy's no thief!" Dannie said, facing off with Wes. "Say he is and I'll knock you down myself!"

Wes's eyes flickered nervously from Dannie to Billy. There was a tense silence.

"Billy's not like that," Alice Ann said.

Billy turned to stare at her. Was Alice Ann actually sticking up for him? Billy Cole? The boy she hated most in all of Scenic?

"Well, you're not!" Alice Ann said, shrugging. "You're rude, and you don't listen, and you play pranks and get in hot water with Miss Wrigley and Mr. Farnam more than anyone else in school. But I don't believe you would take stuff. Really steal, I mean."

Billy felt an embarrassed heat rise to his cheeks. "I, um…well, maybe we can figure out who *did* take those things," he said quickly. "My friends and I are good at solving mysteries."

"Sure! Maybe there are clues!" Finn said. "Let's get a flashlight and take a look around."

"I'll get one." Billy was relieved to have an excuse to get away. When he returned with his father's flashlight, Alice Ann and the others were still jabbering away. They paid no attention as Billy, Finn, Mim, and Dannie walked over to the Lockharts' cabin.

"What kind of clues are we looking for, Billy?" Mim asked.

"Beats me," Billy admitted. "Anything unusual, I guess."

He stepped around his mother, Mrs. Lockhart, and some of the other ladies. It was almost completely dark now. Electric lights inside the Lockharts' cabin sent a yellow glow out through the windows and lit up the evergreens that stood close behind the cabin.

"No wonder no one saw who did it," Dannie said.

"Alice Ann's cabin is right next to the trees. And the Rileys' cabin, too. Someone could have come through the woods and snuck in a back window."

"Shine the light around, Billy," said Finn.

Slowly and carefully Billy made his way toward the back of the cabin. He moved the flashlight beam across the ground and over the cabin's pine walls. Mim, Dannie, and Finn walked alongside, watching closely.

"These pine needles are too thick. Shoes don't leave any prints," Mim said.

"Mmm," Billy agreed. Now that night had fallen, the air had turned bitter cold. Mim wrapped her new scarf more snugly around her throat. Handing the flashlight over to Finn, Billy did the same.

"Hey! I found something!" Finn exclaimed softly.

He dropped to his knees and bent close to the ground. A moment later he held up a squashed, half-burned stub of tobacco wrapped in paper. The sharp smell made Billy wrinkle up his nose in distaste.

"It's a cigarette," he said.

"Store-bought," Dannie added. "See? The brand name is printed right on the paper. Old Gold."

"I bet the thief smoked that!" Finn said. "Who else would be lurking around out here?"

Billy bit his lip, thinking. "But how are we going to figure out who it was? There are plenty of folks in camp who smoke these. Ernie Oliver even has an ad for them tacked up inside the store," he said.

His own parents didn't like cigarettes. But Billy had seen lots of men who did smoke. Some women, too.

"Maybe there's some other clue back here," Mim suggested.

They finished circling the cabin. Then they shined the flashlight around the Rileys' cabin next door.

"Nothing," Billy said.

Disappointed, he stepped into the clearing. His flashlight beam flickered across the front of his own family's cabin. There, hanging from the railing outside the door, was the string of trout Mim and Dannie had caught.

The sight of the glistening, speckled trout startled Billy. With all the fuss over the thefts, he'd almost forgotten about losing the contest.

Almost.

* * *

"How are we going to pick a thief out of all these folks?" Mim groaned. "Practically everyone in camp is here!"

Two hours had passed since Billy had learned about the thefts. The fish fry was well underway. An enormous bonfire crackled in the clearing between the recreation hall and the cookhouse.

Billy's father tended one of the handheld grills. His mother and the other ladies carried cooked trout to the tables that had been set up in the clearing. Billy kept hearing plenty of talk about the thefts. No one seemed to have any idea who was responsible.

"We haven't seen anyone suspicious yet, and we've been watching folks for a while," Billy sighed.

He, Dannie, Mim, and Finn had already eaten their fill of fish. They'd had plenty of the bread, cabbage, potatoes, and pies that Chef Whitman's crew kept bringing from the cookhouse, too. Now the four of them stood next to the recreation hall, looking out at the crowd. They had thought they might find some clue to who had taken Mr. Lockhart's coat and the other things. But now they weren't so sure.

"We might as well give up for now and play tag with everyone else," Dannie said.

Boys and girls were chasing each other at the edge of the clearing. Billy saw that Wes Gundy was "It." He chased Alice Ann, Lucy, and Janet beneath the raised walkway that stretched between the cookhouse and the recreation hall. Wes tagged Alice Ann, and it was her turn to become "It."

Billy was about to join the game when he heard a

familiar voice ask, "Has everyone forgotten about the moving picture?"

Looking up, Billy saw his teacher, Mr. Farnam, standing on the platform outside the recreation hall. His thick brown hair was slicked back from his forehead. Mr. Farnam wore only a sweater over his shirt and tie, but Billy knew he didn't mind the cold. When he wasn't teaching, he spent long hours hiking and trapping on the mountainside above Scenic.

"Need help setting up the projector, Mr. Farnam?" Billy offered.

Their teacher always ran the projector for the Saturday moving picture. More often than not, Billy, Finn, and Dannie helped him.

"Sure. I could use an extra pair of hands," Mr. Farnam answered with a smile.

"Great! Come on, Mim," Dannie said.

The two girls hustled past Billy and Finn. They ran up the stairs and through the recreation hall door without even glancing at Billy or Finn.

They're acting as if we aren't even here! Billy thought. He felt his anger over the marble game and the fishing contest come rushing back.

"Are you two coming?" Mr. Farnam asked. He paused with the door open, glancing down at Finn and Billy.

Billy kicked at the ground with his boot. "I guess you've got all the help you need," he mumbled. "Mim's probably better at it than me, anyhow."

Finn raised his eyebrows. Up on the walkway, Mr. Farnam scratched his head. "Well, suit yourselves, boys," he said. He went inside, and the door shut behind him.

"What'd you say that for?" Finn asked.

Billy shoved his hands in the pockets of his knickers and said nothing.

"I thought running machines was boys' work," Alice Ann spoke up. She and Lucy and Janet had stopped their game to listen. "But I guess tomboys like Dannie and Mim can handle that dirty projector."

"Guess so," Billy said.

Finn's mouth dropped open. Lucy, Janet, and Alice Ann all giggled.

Billy wasn't sure why he'd agreed with Alice Ann. He was usually the first to stick up for his friends. But this time he didn't care.

"Let's get some cookies," he said to Finn.

Finn gave Billy a funny look. "Are you all right?" he asked. "How come you—?"

Finn suddenly stumbled as someone elbowed past him. It was Wes's big brother, Eddie. He had the same round face and black hair as Wes, but he was at least a head taller. He strode over to Wes and teasingly twisted his arm behind his back.

"Ow!" Wes complained. "Where were you all after-noon?"

"None of your beeswax, runt," Eddie answered.

Billy leaned toward Finn. "Hey, I don't remember seeing Eddie after we found out about those things being stolen from the cabins. Do you?"

Finn nodded. "And now he won't tell Wes where he was. Do you think he…," he began.

Billy glanced over his shoulder. Eddie was still play wrestling with Wes. "I don't know," he said. "Guess we'd better keep an eye on him from now on."

"*After* we get cookies," Finn said, grinning.

He and Billy made their way through the crowd to the cookhouse. They went up the wooden stairs, then followed the raised walkway to the back of the building. Children weren't allowed in the cookhouse—it was just for the men who worked inside the tunnel. But Chef Whitman's bakers usually didn't mind giving handouts.

Billy pulled the back door open. Right away his mouth began to water. "I smell sugar cookies," he said.

Finn glanced past the vats and supplies that filled the back of the cookhouse. "Looks like Chef Whitman's having some kind of meeting," he whispered.

Onions, meat, knives, and potatoes lay on the counter in front of them. Dirty pans were piled in the sinks, but the kitchen area was empty. Billy could see that the cooks were all at the front of the cookhouse. They clustered around one of the long tables where workers usually took their meals. Chef Whitman stood talking to them, his apron stretched tight across his large middle.

"No need to bother them," Billy whispered. Grinning, he tiptoed toward the cooling racks. Half a dozen trays of cookies filled one of them. "No one will mind if we sneak just a few."

He and Finn crouched low so the counter would hide them. But as Billy reached for a cookie, his elbow bumped against a stack of tin plates on the counter. They hit the floor with a deafening clatter.

The next thing Billy knew, Chef Whitman was yanking him to his feet. One of the bakers had Finn by the arm. A sea of men in white aprons scowled at them.

"You two! Well, I never would have expected it," Chef Whitman said. "It looks like Scenic's thief is Mr. Cole's own boy!"

CHAPTER FOUR

CAUGHT RED-HANDED

A thief? *Me?*" Billy squeaked. He tried to push back the panic that leaped into his throat. "I—I didn't steal anything!"

Chef Whitman pointed to the trays of cookies in their rack. "You were about to. Don't deny it. Now tell me what you did with the chickens!"

Finn stared blankly at Chef Whitman. "Chickens?" he asked.

"Three of them," the chef said firmly.

What's going on here? Billy wondered. He and Finn had snuck cookies dozens of times before. Chef Whitman had never made such a fuss over it.

"We heard about the money and all that was taken from the family cabins, too," said the young baker who had grabbed Finn. Billy remembered his name was Gil. "You boys are in big trouble."

All at once, Billy understood. "Wait! You think *we* stole all that stuff? We didn't!" he said.

"Well, maybe a few cookies. But that's all," Finn added sheepishly. He twisted around to face Billy. "Gee, that's a lot of stolen loot now, Billy! Mr. Lockhart's coat, a pie, Mr. Riley's binoculars, ten dollars...."

"And now three chickens from the cookhouse," Billy finished.

"It's more than that," Gil said. "Add a couple loaves of bread. And some beef that was to go in tomorrow's stew."

"Criminy. So do you think it was the same person who took it all, Chef Whitman?" Billy asked. "It sure wasn't us."

The big man's expression softened. He let go of Billy and rubbed the unshaved stubble on his chin. "You know, no thief would ask as many questions as you two. Maybe I was hasty to accuse you. But from now on," he said, wagging a fat finger at the boys, "no sneaking around. Got it?"

"Got it," Billy said. He and Finn both nodded.

Chef Whitman slid a handful of cookies off the cooling rack and handed them to the boys. "Next time you want a snack, you come and ask for it."

"Yes, sir!" Billy and Finn answered together.

* * *

By the time the boys went back outside, the bonfire for the fish fry was dying down. Billy's mother and the other women from the Scenic Ladies Society were collecting casserole dishes and piling up tin plates to return to the cookhouse. Eddie, Wes, and the other kids were heading into the recreation hall.

"Looks like folks are going to the moving picture," Finn said. "I heard Mr. Farnam say it's *The Adventures of Rin Tin Tin*."

"Yeah, let's go," said Billy. He crammed the last cookie into his mouth.

"Maybe we'll see someone at the picture wearing Mr. Lockhart's missing coat," said Finn. "Or Mr. Riley's binoculars."

"Mm-hmm," said Billy, swallowing. " And we can keep an eye on Eddie, too."

"Shouldn't we tell Dannie and Mim about the chickens and things missing from the cookhouse?" Finn added.

"All right," Billy agreed.

But as soon as he saw Mim helping to thread the film through the sprockets of the projector, Billy felt annoyed all over again.

"Okay, Finn. You tell Mim and Dannie," he said, scowling. Steering clear of the girls, Billy headed for the front row to sit by himself.

The lights went down and the picture began. Billy kept his eyes on Eddie and his friend Jim, who were sitting a few seats over. The two just sat and watched the picture. They weren't acting very suspicious.

Billy turned his attention to Rin Tin Tin, the famous dog on the screen. He forgot all about Mim and Dannie until the picture was over. The girls hurried over to him as soon as the lights came on. Billy's sister Marjorie stood between them, holding their hands.

"Finn just told us what happened at the cookhouse," Mim said.

"So there are even *more* stolen things to look for now," Dannie added. She glanced left and right at men and women putting on their coats and moving toward the door. "We could keep an eye on folks right now! Maybe someone has a bundle of loot right here with them."

"Can I help?" Marjorie asked, looking up at Dannie and Mim.

"Gee, I wish you could. But I promised Aunt Ruth I'd get you home right away," Mim said.

She shot a quick glance at Billy. Was she waiting for him to offer to go with them? Or ask them to stay? Billy just shrugged and said, "See you later."

"*I'll* go with you, Mim," Dannie offered. She glared at Billy over Marjorie's head. "Come on."

Billy pretended he didn't notice the hurt expression on his cousin's face. After all, she deserved it.

Didn't she?

Billy and Finn spent the next half hour standing next to the recreation hall door. They didn't see anyone carrying binoculars or any suspicious-looking sack. Plenty of men wore black overcoats, but they all looked the same to Billy. He didn't have any idea how to tell which coat might belong to Mr. Lockhart.

At last he and Finn gave up and went home.

"Shh! Your sister's already asleep," Billy's mother said as he stepped into the kitchen. A pile of folded blankets and sheets sat on the table next to Mrs. Cole's mending basket. "Take these to make up a bed for yourself," she added.

Billy had forgotten that Mim would be sleeping in his bed. She always did when she visited. When he climbed the stairs to the attic, she was lying on his bed writing in her diary. The five-dollar bill she had won in the fishing contest was tacked up on the windowsill behind her.

Mim must have seen him frowning at it. Shutting her diary, she pulled the tack and held out the money to Billy.

"Here. We can share it. "You're the one who taught me how to fish in the first place."

She wasn't acting at all smug now. Billy felt himself soften. "You won it fair and square," he said. Marjorie's rhythmic breathing came from her bed on the far side of the loft. Billy began laying out the blankets on the floor. Mim jumped up to help.

"I, um…I'm sorry if I made you feel bad, Billy. I didn't mean to," she said.

Billy shook his head. "All you did was get better at fishing. And marbles. I guess that's nothing to be sorry for."

He smiled, and Mim grinned back.

"Did you see anyone with Mr. Riley's binoculars?" she asked. "Or Mr. Lockhart's overcoat?"

Billy shook his head. "No," he said. "But Finn and I noticed something else. Eddie Gundy didn't show up at the fish fry 'til it was almost over…."

He told Mim the whole story. It was good to feel that they were on the same side again.

"So now we need to figure out if he's the thief," Mim said when Billy had finished. "But how?"

All at once she snapped her fingers. "Maybe it'll help if we write down everything we know," she said.

"Sure!" Billy grabbed a pencil from his pile of school-books. Mim ripped an empty page from her diary.

Sitting side by side on Billy's bed, they went to work.

Chapter Five

CLUE ON THE MOUNTAIN

"So we're looking for someone who steals food, clothes, and money," Dannie said. "That could be anyone."

It was Monday morning. Mim, Marjorie, and Billy had just caught up to Dannie and Finn on the path to the schoolhouse. The first thing Billy did was show his friends the list he and Mim had made. They hadn't seen Finn and Dannie since the moving picture on Saturday night. Billy's family and Mim had spent Sunday in Skykomish, the closest real town to Scenic.

Finn took the list from Billy and held it up so they could all see.

WHAT	WHEN	WHERE
coat	Sat	Lockharts
pie	Sat	Lockharts
binoculars	Sat	Rileys
$10	Sat	Rileys
3 chickens	Sat	cookhouse
bread	Sat	cookhouse
beef	Sat	cookhouse

CLUES:
* Old Gold cigarette behind Lockharts' cabin
* Eddie Gundy wasn't at fishing contest and arrived late to fish fry—wouldn't say where he was.

"Maybe a drifter did it," Finn suggested. "You know, someone who doesn't have anyplace to live or money for food."

"A drifter would need food and a coat," Billy agreed. He shivered, remembering the feeling he'd had in the woods that someone was watching him.

"But there isn't anyone like that in Scenic," Dannie pointed out. "Anyhow, what would a drifter want with binoculars?"

Billy didn't know. "It doesn't make sense that Eddie would take that stuff, either. He has a place to live, and plenty of food."

"Well, if he wasn't doing anything wrong, why wouldn't he tell Wes where he was on Saturday?" said Finn. "Maybe Eddie took those things out of plain meanness."

"Maybe," Billy said. He took the list from Finn and slipped it back into the pocket of his knickers. "We can't know for sure until we find out more."

When they reached the schoolhouse, Mim and Marjorie went into the classroom where Miss Wrigley taught students in grades one through four. Just the year before, Finn, Billy, and Dannie had been in Miss Wrigley's class, too. Now that they were in fifth grade, Mr. Farnam was their teacher. He taught grades five through eight.

Billy was glad for the change. Mr. Farnam wasn't nearly as strict as Miss Wrigley. He didn't seem to care as much about rules and proper behavior, either. He even kept handbills for local wrestling and boxing matches tacked up beneath the photographs of the United States presidents.

When Billy stepped into the classroom, the teacher was leaning back in his chair with his boots propped on his desk. A dozen iron traps were piled on the floor next to him. He was holding one in his hand, rubbing it all over with a grease-drenched cloth.

"See that?" Finn whispered excitedly.

Billy knew Mr. Farnam trapped martens in the winter for their fur. A few times last year, he had even cut out lessons and taken his class up the mountain to check his traps. Billy and Finn had watched longingly from Miss Wrigley's class.

The other students were filing into the classroom. Billy saw the doubtful way Alice Ann and her friends Lucy and Janet stared at the traps.

"Shouldn't you have our lesson books out instead of those smelly traps?" Alice Ann asked. She wrinkled up her nose as she sat at her desk in the fifth-grade row.

Mr. Farnam laughed. "There are more ways to learn than just from books, Alice Ann," he said, setting down his trap. "Today we're going to hike up the mountain to learn how Mother Nature prepares for winter."

"And scout out where to place his traps this winter, I bet," Dannie whispered.

"Who cares? We're going!" said Billy. Then he thought of Mim. "Mr. Farnam?" he called out. "Can Miss Wrigley's class come, too?"

A broad smile spread across his teacher's face. "Why, that's a fine idea, Billy. I'll ask her right now," he said. He slicked back his hair and got to his feet. "Class, you may hand in your grammar assignments and then wait at your desks."

"I didn't do mine," Eddie called from the back of the seventh-grade row. "I was too busy."

Eddie's friend Jim rolled his eyes. "Busy goofing off, you mean," he said. "I saw you go off into the woods yesterday after Reverend Silsby's service."

"And *I* got stuck doing his chores," Wes grumbled, scowling at his big brother. "He cut out without saying a word to anyone. Didn't come back 'til suppertime."

Billy caught the excited glances Finn and Dannie shot at him. So Eddie had gone off a *second* time without any explanation!

"Where'd you go, Eddie?" Billy asked casually.

Eddie made a face at him. "Wouldn't you like to know," he said. "Mind your own business."

"That's enough squabbling," Mr. Farnam spoke up. He shot a warning glance at Eddie from the doorway. "I'll speak with you later about your assignment. Being busy is no excuse."

* * *

As they set off up the mountain, Billy kept his eye on Eddie. But soon he forgot about everything except how happy he was to be outside on such a clear, sunny day.

The air was cold. Mim's cheeks were as red as her

scarf. But no one seemed to mind. Even Alice Ann seemed interested as Mr. Farnam pointed out spots where cougars, bears, and bobcats had scraped the bark from the trunks of the fir trees. He showed them lichens and ferns that the deer and elk would eat once the last of the Cascades grapes were gone. He pointed out caves that might be home to hibernating bears. And he spoke of the Indian tribes that had once fished, hunted, and foraged for berries in the Cascades.

"Of course, the natives always left the mountain before the snows hit," Mr. Farnam told them. "They moved to winter villages farther downstream."

"Which tribes?" Mim asked. "The Skykomish?"

Mr. Farnam gave an impressed nod. "Right you are," he told her.

"Didn't I see a book about the Skykomish in your classroom, Mr. Farnam?" Miss Wrigley asked. "Perhaps you'll be kind enough to show it to Mim."

She smiled at him, and several of the girls giggled. Billy rolled his eyes. Those girls always whispered whenever a look or smile passed between the two teachers.

"Look at that beaver dam!" Mim cried.

Crystal Lake had just come into view. Ahead of them Billy saw the falls that spilled into the Tye River.

Beyond them, in a protected curve of the lake, was a large dome of sticks and mud. The dam had been there all summer. But it was a good three feet thicker and higher now than it had been.

"Guess the beavers are ready for winter," Mr. Farnam said. "They've been building up these walls to keep the cold out. Critters always seem to know better than men when winter's going to hit hard." He tilted his head back and gazed beyond the treetops. "Sky's clear now, but I wouldn't be surprised if an early storm hits this year."

"And Father doesn't even have a winter coat," Alice Ann said.

"There's bound to be someone in camp with a coat he can have or use," Miss Wrigley reassured her.

"I suppose," Alice Ann said, frowning. "But I'd feel better if Mr. Jenkins and the police caught whoever took it. Coats are expensive, you know."

"Well, whoever took it could be anywhere," Lucy said. "Maybe right in Scenic. How do we know he won't steal again?"

Billy glanced over his shoulder at Eddie. He was clowning around with Jim and didn't seem to have heard the girls.

But Marjorie had heard. She looked up at Miss

Wrigley with wide eyes. "I want to go home," she said in a trembling voice.

Miss Wrigley crouched down and put an arm around Marjorie. "Don't you worry. We're far from any trouble here," she said. "And it's so lovely here by the lake. Why don't we stop for lunch? We might even have time for a few games before we go back to school."

* * *

"Children! It's time to leave!" Miss Wrigley called out some time later.

Billy and the other kids were playing hide-and-seek in the woods next to Crystal Lake. Even Marjorie had joined in and seemed to have forgotten about being afraid. Billy's cheeks were almost numb from so many hours spent in the cold. He kept blowing on his hands to warm them. Still, he and Finn didn't return to the group right away.

"Let's find Mim first," Finn said.

Billy nodded. "You go that way," he said, pointing left. "I'll go right."

Mim was one of the few kids on the other team who hadn't yet been found. Billy circled around some fir trees, then scanned the steep, rocky slope beyond. Two slabs of rock were set into the hillside. They leaned against each other at an angle. Billy peered at the dark triangle of shadow between them.

"A cave?" he murmured.

It was just the kind of place where Mim might hide. *Or where a grizzly might hibernate,* Billy reminded himself. He approached the cave cautiously.

All he saw at first was darkness. There was a burned smell in the air, as if someone had made a fire. As Billy drew closer to the rocks, he could make out the silhouette of something lumpy inside the cave. It looked too soft to be rock. Maybe…a blanket?

"Or Mr. Lockhart's coat!" he whispered to himself.

He took a step closer. It looked like heavy fabric, all right. Was that a sleeve he saw folded on top? Yes!

Just as Billy reached toward it, a scream rang through the air. He jumped back, startled.

"Finn!" Billy called. "Someone's in trouble!"

Chapter Six

STRANGER AMONG THE TREES

Heart pounding, Billy ran back the way he had come. Finn was racing straight toward him from the other direction.

"I think that scream came from near the lake," Finn said. "Let's go!"

He and Billy hurried as fast as they could over the matted pine needles that covered the ground. With fir trees so thick around them, they couldn't see Crystal Lake. But Billy heard the alarmed cries of their classmates. By the time they reached the water, boys and girls were crowded next to a boulder near the water's edge. Dannie and Buster came running up at the same time.

"What happened?" Dannie cried.

Alice Ann sat on the boulder hugging her knees.

Tears streamed down her cheeks. Miss Wrigley was trying to comfort her. But Billy saw the scared way Alice Ann's eyes darted around.

"He was h—hiding in the trees, Miss Wrigley," Alice Ann said. "Right over there!"

She pointed at a thick clump of pines behind her. Mr. Farnam was already circling around the trees.

"Well, he's gone now," he said, rejoining the group.

"Who? Who did you see?" asked Billy.

A shadow crossed Alice Ann's face. "A man. He was hiding there, watching us," she said.

"I saw something, too," Billy began. "There was a—"

"You're sure it wasn't Mr. Farnam?" Dannie cut in. "He and Miss Wrigley were playing hide-and-seek with everyone, too."

Alice Ann frowned at Dannie. "Don't you think I know our own teacher? This was a *stranger,*" she insisted. "He ran away when I screamed. Mr. Farnam wouldn't do that."

"No, he certainly wouldn't," Miss Wrigley agreed.

"I saw something strange, too," Billy repeated, louder this time. He elbowed past his classmates and stepped closer to Alice Ann and Miss Wrigley. "A cave. It looks like someone might be living there. I think I saw a—"

"Oww!"

A loud groan interrupted him.

"My ankle...." Mim limped forward from the trees. She was the last one to rejoin the group.

No wonder it took her so long, thought Billy. Every time she tried to put weight on her left foot, her face twisted with pain.

"Mim! What happened?" cried Billy. He and Dannie hurried to help her.

"I was running back after I heard the scream," Mim began. "But I fell, and...well, I think I've sprained my ankle."

Mr. Farnam crouched down and gently touched Mim's ankle. "There's no swelling yet. But we'd better get you back to camp right away and ice it up."

"What about the cave Billy found?" said Alice Ann. "That strange man I saw might still be lurking around!" She bit her lip, glancing left and right. "Shouldn't we try to find out what he's doing?"

"Maybe Buster can track him," Dannie offered. She patted her dog's silky head, but Mim just groaned louder.

"It hurts *sooo* much," she said, clutching her ankle.

Billy saw Mr. Farnam and Miss Wrigley exchange worried looks.

"We need to get Mim to camp right away," Mr. Farnam said. "But I'll come back later this afternoon and take a look around myself."

That seemed to satisfy Alice Ann. But not Mim. She frowned as she limped along the path between the teacher and Dannie.

"Couldn't you come here tomorrow, Mr. Farnam? I was hoping you'd show me your book about the Skykomish Indians," Mim said.

"But Mim," Billy protested, "what if that was Mr. Lockhart's stolen coat I saw in the cave? Mr. Farnam might be able to find out who the thief is. Maybe even catch him!"

Mim winced as she took another limping step. "Maybe Alice Ann didn't really see anyone," she said. "No one else saw any strange man."

Billy could hardly believe his ears. The fear in Alice Ann's scream had been real—he was sure of it. But Mim was making it sound as if Alice Ann had made the whole thing up!

"I did so see someone!" Alice Ann insisted.

"That's enough, children!" Miss Wrigley said firmly. She held Marjorie and another first-grade girl by the hand. "Now let's head back to camp."

"I don't suppose it'll make any difference if I wait 'til tomorrow to look around," Mr. Farnam said slowly. "Alice Ann's scream probably scared away whoever she saw. I'll stop by your cabin later with that book, Mim."

Relief spread across Mim's face. "Thanks, Mr. Farnam," she said.

Billy frowned. He almost had the feeling that Mim wanted to make sure Mr. Farnam *didn't* go back up the mountain.

As soon as the thought crossed his mind, Billy shook it away. *That's crazy,* he told himself.

Still, Mim was acting a little...different. Billy was used to his cousin's steady chatter. Now she barely said a word. And she wouldn't meet his gaze.

She wasn't any more talkative at home, either. Mim sat on the sofa writing furiously in her diary while Billy's mother fussed over her.

"Can you move it, honey?" Mrs. Cole asked, bringing ice wrapped in a towel for Mim's ankle.

"A little," Mim said.

But when Billy came back from taking the garbage to the trash heap, Mim was *outside* the cabin. She barely limped as she climbed the steps to go back inside. In fact, she didn't seem to be limping at all.

"Hey, Mim!" Billy called. "How'd your ankle get better so fast?"

Mim whirled around. "Oh! It, uh...I guess all that

ice Aunt Ruth put on it did the trick," she said.

Billy stared at her. Why was his cousin acting so nervous? So…guilty? "Where'd you go?" he asked.

"No place special," she told him. Turning her back, she hurried inside.

Billy followed. It wasn't until he stepped into the main room that he noticed the empty space behind the cabin door.

"Hey! My rod's gone," he said. "Mother! Have you seen my new fishing rod? I left it right here."

"Your mother's not here. She took Marjorie over to the store to buy some flour and things," Mim said.

Billy searched the cabin from top to bottom, but he didn't find the rod. "It's gone," he said. "Someone took it!"

"Are you sure you didn't leave it someplace else?" Mim asked. Again, Billy noticed that she didn't look him in the eye.

"It was right here. I *know* it was," he insisted.

Mim grabbed her diary from the sofa and hurried toward the kitchen. It seemed to Billy as if she couldn't wait to get away from him.

But why?

Billy watched her climb the stairs to the attic. Her limp had completely disappeared.

No hurt ankle heals that fast, he thought.

Then a question popped into his head and stuck there like tar.

Had Mim *faked* being hurt? Had she pretended to sprain her ankle so they would all have to leave the mountain? Had she done it to keep Mr. Farnam from seeing the cave Billy had found?

And now his rod was missing, too.

Billy dropped down into a chair at the kitchen table. Reaching into the pocket of his knickers, he pulled out the list he and Mim had made. He grabbed the pencil his mother always kept on the counter to write down things she needed to buy at the store, and added these words to his list:

What	*When*	*Where*
fishing rod	*Mon*	*our cabin*

Under clues, he wrote:

* *Saw coat in cave by Crystal Lake*
* *Alice Ann saw strange man near lake*

He sighed, then quickly scrawled four new clues:

* *Mim wanted people away from the cave*
* *She was alone in our cabin before I found my rod missing*
* *She went out by herself and wouldn't say where she went*
* *She's acting funny*

Billy didn't like what he was thinking. Not one bit. But he couldn't ignore it, either. At the bottom of his paper, he wrote one more thing:

Is Mim the thief?

Chapter Seven
SUSPICIONS

Billy awoke Tuesday morning to find Marjorie bent over him in her nightgown. Her eyes were sleepy and her hair was tousled. Billy saw a crease along her cheek where she'd slept on a seam of her pillow.

"Where's Mim?" Marjorie asked.

"Hmm?" Yawning, Billy sat up on his bed of blankets. Sure enough, Mim wasn't in the attic. She had straightened out the blanket of Billy's bed and pulled the coverlet neatly over the pillow.

Billy tried to push aside his uneasiness. "Maybe she's helping with breakfast," he said.

But when they went down to the kitchen, their mother was alone at the stove. There was a note on the table in Mim's handwriting:

Dear Aunt Ruth and Uncle James,

Went for a walk before school. Please don't worry.

Love,
Mim

Billy scowled at the words. They didn't say very much. "Where'd she go so early?" he mumbled.

"Oh, you know Mim," his mother said lightly. She flipped a couple of sputtering eggs in the frying pan. "She's always up to something new."

That was just what Billy was afraid of.

"If I were you," Mrs. Cole went on, "I'd stop worrying about Mim and start trying to find your new fishing rod."

"Okay," was all Billy said. What else could he say? That he was afraid *Mim* might be the one who had taken it? His mother wouldn't believe that for a second. Billy didn't want to believe it himself.

But Mim was keeping some kind of secret. One she wouldn't tell even to him.

Somehow he had to find out what it was.

* * *

"You think Mim *faked* that sprained ankle?" Finn said. "Then she took your new rod?"

Billy nodded. His lunch pail thudded against his leg as the two of them and Dannie walked toward the schoolhouse alongside the river.

"That's a lot of baloney!" Dannie said. "You're just jealous 'cause Mim won that fishing contest instead of you."

Billy kicked at the pine needles on the ground. "Don't you think it's strange that she happened to sprain her ankle right when I told Mr. Farnam about the cave I saw?" he asked. "Then she was moaning while Mother fussed over her. But the second she was alone, her ankle got better. And that's when my fishing rod disappeared!"

"That still doesn't mean she's the one who took it," Dannie pointed out. "Maybe it was missing before and you didn't notice."

"I would have noticed," Billy said.

"You don't think Mim took all those other things, too, do you?" Finn asked. He watched thoughtfully as Buster ran barking toward a kingfisher perched next to the river. "I mean, Mim was with us when the coat and binoculars and things were taken from the family cabins."

"She was with us during the fish fry, too. So she couldn't have taken any chickens or bread or meat," Dannie added. She frowned at Billy. "How can you accuse your own cousin? And she's so nice, too. It isn't right."

Billy didn't like being suspicious of Mim. But he couldn't ignore how he felt. "She's up to something. I know it," he said.

Ahead, the schoolhouse came into sight through the trees. A handful of boys and girls were already in the school yard. Mim wasn't among them.

"Where *is* she?" Billy wondered.

"If you ask me, Mim just doesn't seem like a stealing kind of person," Finn said. "She's not mean like Eddie."

"Speaking of Eddie..." Dannie murmured.

She stopped next to the rail fence that circled the school yard. Climbing onto the lower rail, she peered past the school, toward Lookout Rock. The granite ledge jutted out of the mountainside just above the schoolhouse. Two boys stood on top of the rock. Billy recognized Eddie Gundy's stocky figure and the taller, thinner figure of Eddie's friend Jim.

"Why are they hunched over like that?" Finn said.

Billy saw Eddie flick something against the rock. "He's got a match. Look—he's lighting a cigarette!"

Up on Lookout Rock, both boys immediately doubled over, coughing and gasping. Billy saw Eddie throw down the cigarette and stomp it out with his boot. Still coughing, the two boys came down the steep path toward the school yard. Their faces looked almost green.

"Are you thinking what I'm thinking?" Finn asked Billy and Dannie.

"You mean, about that cigarette we found behind Alice Ann's cabin?" Billy said. "Maybe *Eddie* left it there! Let's go see if the one he's got is the same kind."

They were halfway up the steep path when Billy heard the morning bell. Lessons were about to begin. Still, the three of them kept right on climbing. Seconds later, they clambered out on top of Lookout Rock.

"Over here!" Dannie ran toward the far edge of the rock, where they'd seen Eddie and Jim. Billy and Finn caught up to her just as she picked up the cigarette stub.

The stub was squashed and partly burned. Billy could still make out the tiny gold letters printed on one end.

"See that?" he said. "Old Gold."

Chapter Eight
SNEAKY SUSPECTS

"Criminy!" said Finn, letting out a whistle. "Maybe Eddie *is* the camp thief!"

Dannie turned to Billy with an I-told-you-so look. "*Now* will you admit you were wrong about Mim?" she asked.

"We should definitely find out if Eddie smoked the Old Gold cigarette we found behind Alice Ann's cabin," Billy said. "But I'm still going to keep my eye on Mim." Standing at the edge of Lookout Rock, he gazed out over the Scenic camp. *If she ever turns up,* he added to himself.

When Mim finally did arrive, Billy, Finn, and Dannie were already at their desks. Billy saw her tiptoe through the coatroom and into Miss Wrigley's classroom.

"Eyes on your lesson, Billy," Mr. Farnam warned.

But Billy couldn't concentrate on geography. When Mr. Farnam asked him to name the capital of Minnesota, Billy said *Mim*eapolis instead of Minneapolis. And even though Eddie didn't do anything suspicious or act up any more than usual, Billy kept glancing his way. The minutes dragged on until it was time for the noon-hour recess.

"Finally!" Billy jumped up from his desk and headed for the coatroom. "Let's find out where Mim snuck to this morning," he whispered to Dannie and Finn.

"She didn't sneak," Dannie said. "She just went for a walk."

Billy shrugged. "We'll see about that," he said.

Mim was just coming out of the other classroom. Billy hurried over to her. "So, Mim," he began, "where did you—"

"Guess what?" Mim cut in. She stepped past Billy and smiled at Dannie. "Miss Wrigley wants Marjorie and me to help her unpack the new primers. She said you can help us, Dannie."

"Finn and I will help, too," Billy offered.

Mim glanced nervously at them. "Hmm? Oh— there's no need," she said quickly. "Miss Wrigley asked for just one more person. Here's your sandwich and apple, Billy." She dug into the lunch pail that Billy's mother had packed for them. After handing over his lunch, Mim hurried back into Miss Wrigley's classroom with the pail. Marjorie followed on her heels, but Dannie held back.

Putting her face close to Billy's, she said, "Mim is *not* a sneaky thief!"

Then she, too, disappeared into Miss Wrigley's classroom.

Billy frowned. "Why is Mim in such a hurry to get away from me?" he murmured to Finn.

"Forget about her," Finn said. "Eddie's the one we need to talk to, remember?"

Billy stared back into their classroom. Eddie was talking to Mr. Farnam at the teacher's desk.

"I guess," Billy agreed.

Eddie did *smoke that Old Gold cigarette,* he reminded himself. Moments later, when Eddie put on his jacket and went outside, Billy and Finn followed.

"Hey, Eddie!" Finn called out.

Eddie stopped next to the school yard fence. Just beyond, Jim Walsh and some of the other older boys were eating lunch on the banks of the Tye.

"What do you want?" Eddie asked as Billy and Finn caught up to him.

Eddie was a head taller than Billy—and twice as big

around. Taking a deep breath, Billy faced him squarely.

"Since when do you smoke Old Gold cigarettes?" he demanded.

"None of your beeswax," Eddie said. But Billy saw his eyes dart toward Lookout Rock.

"It is if you're stealing!" Finn said hotly. "Whoever took Mr. Lockhart's coat and all that other stuff smokes cigarettes. Old Golds, just like you."

Eddie stared at Finn. "You think *I* took that junk?" he said. Then he threw back his head and laughed. "That's a good one!"

Billy frowned. If Eddie was guilty, he sure wasn't acting like it. "It's not funny, Eddie. You're going to be in big trouble if we prove you're the thief," he said.

"Yeah? Go ahead and try," Eddie shot back. He gave Billy a hard shove and stormed away.

Billy straightened his jacket. *Was that a denial—or a dare?* he wondered.

No matter how many times he went over Eddie's words in his mind, Billy couldn't be sure.

* * *

"Where's Mim going *now?*" Billy said under his breath.

Mr. Farnam had just rung the end-of-day bell. Billy quickly grabbed his coat, but Mim was faster. By the time Billy left the schoolhouse with Dannie and Finn, Mim was already scrambling up the path above Lookout Rock.

"Will you stop wasting your time trying to prove Mim's up to no good?" Dannie said. She shot an irritated glance at Billy. Then she whistled for Buster, who came running from the trees beyond the school yard. "Come on, boy. We've got laundry to do."

Billy knew that Dannie didn't have a mother at home. Her mother had died before Mr. Renwick brought Dannie and her big brother to Scenic. Many afternoons Dannie was stuck with the household chores. As she headed for the cabins, Billy glanced back up the mountainside.

Mim's red scarf was getting smaller. Soon the evergreens would hide her completely.

"I'm going to see where she's going," Billy said to Finn.

He started toward the path, then glanced over his shoulder at his friend. Finn stayed where he was.

"What about Eddie? Shouldn't we keep an eye on him?" Finn asked.

"Suit yourself," Billy said, shrugging. "I'm going after Mim."

Leaving Finn in the school yard, he climbed up to Lookout Rock. Mim's scarf was a dot of red far ahead of him. She was moving fast. Billy had to hustle to keep her in sight.

Mim kept to the old Indian trail along the river. She didn't turn off the path until she reached Crystal Lake. Then she headed north, into the woods.

Straight toward the cave I found! Billy thought.

He picked up his pace, but paused when Mim stopped in her tracks. Billy ducked behind the branches of a fir tree about twenty yards back.

What's she up to? he wondered.

Mim glanced around, and then doubled back toward the lake. Had she seen him? Billy held his breath. To his relief, Mim didn't come all the way back to where he was hiding. She turned onto the path that circled Crystal Lake. Keeping his distance, Billy followed.

The path wound in and out of the trees. Peering out, Billy saw a hawk soaring above. Some water voles scurried into their burrow on the bank. Up ahead, two black-tailed deer drank from the water. They bounded away as Mim approached. She climbed onto a log that stretched from the edge of the lake to a rocky, tree-covered island.

Billy knew that island well. He, Finn, and Dannie had explored it many times. It was tiny—less than a hundred feet long and half as wide. Fir trees, wild roses, and grapevines grew so thick that it was impossible to see from one end to the other. As soon as Mim disappeared into the thick mass of branches, Billy scrambled across the log after her.

A narrow path led through the tangle of trees and vines. He didn't see his cousin, but he knew she couldn't be far away. Billy moved quickly down the path, peering left and right.

"Mim?" he called.

There was no answer. Billy heard branches rustling, but he couldn't see Mim.

"I know you're here. Come talk to me!" he said.

Just then Billy heard a loud grunt somewhere behind him. It was followed by the smack of something hitting the water.

He whirled around, racing back the way he had come. Thorny rose vines clung to his jacket and scarf. He burst from the trees and skidded to a stop on the rocks that edged the island.

Floating in the water, just out of reach, was the log bridge. It was the only way on or off the island.

He was stranded.

Chapter Nine

TRICKED!

Mim!" Billy shouted.

She was hurrying northward through the trees. But when she heard Billy, she looked back over her shoulder.

"That's what you get for sneaking after me!" she called. Then she circled around a fir tree and was gone from sight.

Billy was steaming mad. How could Mim trick him like this?

Well, you were *following her,* said a tiny voice at the back of his head. Billy shook it away.

Climbing down the rocky bank, he dipped his hand in the water. "Brrr!" he said, yanking it out again. The water was so cold it felt like a thousand needles pricking his skin. He'd freeze to death if he tried to swim across!

Now what? he wondered.

Frowning, Billy gazed into the tangle of trees, vines, and thorns. That was when he heard it. A voice in the distance.

It wasn't Mim's. But it was a voice he knew just as well.

"Finn!" Billy shouted. "Over here!"

Finn appeared on the trail a moment later. His wild hair looked even redder than usual in the afternoon light. He ran around the lake until he reached the shore opposite Billy.

"Jeepers!" Finn said, shaking his head. "It's a good thing I changed my mind and came to find you. What happened?"

"Don't ask," Billy muttered. "Just help me off here so we can find Mim!"

* * *

"Okay, Billy. I've got her steady," Finn said a few minutes later.

Finn had managed to get hold of the fallen log bridge floating in the lake when it drifted near the shore. He had nearly fallen in himself trying to push the end across to where Billy waited on the island. After many tries, Billy had finally dragged his end of the log onto the rocks. Now, while Finn held it in place, Billy made his way carefully across.

"We did it!" he crowed as he stepped to solid ground.

Letting go of the log, Finn stood up and stared out into the trees. "Now all we have to do is find Mim," he said. "I guess you were right about her, Billy. She *must* be hiding something if she tricked you into getting stuck here."

"Well, I'm not beat yet. Not by a long shot," Billy said. He started north through the woods. "The cave I found yesterday is this way. I bet anything that's where Mim went."

This time Finn didn't hesitate. Together they retraced their steps to the place near the lake where they had played hide-and-seek the day before.

The sun was dipping lower in the sky. Billy banged his arms against his sides to keep them warm. He knew they would have to move fast in order to reach the cave and get back to camp before dark.

"There!" Billy pointed past a clump of fir trees to a rocky hillside. Set into the hillside were the two slabs of rock that formed an upside-down V. "That's the entrance to the cave," he said.

Finn bit his lip. "You think Mim's in there?" he said doubtfully.

Pushing aside his own nervousness, Billy moved closer. He ducked beneath the rocks and peered inside the cave.

"Mim?" he called softly.

He blinked until his eyes adjusted to the darkness. All he saw were the rock walls and dirt floor of the cave. There was no coat now—or anything else. Billy moved slowly around the cave, brushing his hands all around. He still found nothing.

"She's not here. The cave's empty," he said. He brushed dirt from his hands as he came out into the light again. "But it wasn't empty yesterday. I'm sure I saw a coat!"

His nose was tickled by the same burned, smoky odor he'd smelled the day before. "Someone built a fire, too. Can you smell it?"

Finn was crouching next to the ground about ten feet away. "It was right here," he said.

Pine needles had been cleared from the ground in front of Finn. Billy saw stubs of burned logs inside a ring of rocks. There were dark smudges on the rocks. Bending closer, Billy saw that someone had made drawings with a charred bit of wood. Each drawing was the same—a stick figure hanging from a gallows.

"Ugh," Billy said, making a face. "Do you think Mim made those? And why would she build a fire?"

"Beats me," said Finn. "But she came this way after she left you on that island, right?"

"And yesterday she faked a sprained ankle to keep Mr. Farnam from looking around here," Billy added. "But where is she *now?*"

He turned, taking in the trees and rocks and evergreens. Juncos and squirrels jabbered noisily among the trees. But he still saw no sign of Mim.

"Hey, look!" Finn said.

He straightened up from the rocks of the campfire. Pinched between his thumb and forefinger was a piece of red yarn.

"Looks like this caught on some splintered rock," he said.

Taking the yarn, Billy held it against his own scarf. It matched perfectly.

"I bet it's from Mim's scarf!" he said. He unwound his scarf and looked it over. "See? There aren't any snags or holes in mine. So this *must* have come from Mim's!"

"She was here, all right," Finn said. As he stepped away from the ring of rocks, he shook something off his boot. Finn glanced down—and gasped. "Billy, look what else is here!"

Billy's jaw dropped. It was a tangled knot of fishing line! "So Mim *did* take my new rod," he said.

"But why?" Finn asked. "What was she doing here? Why isn't she here now? And where's your rod?"

All Billy could do was shrug. "Something strange is going on for sure," he said. "And Mim is right in the middle of it."

Chapter Ten
Mim's Secret

"Where's Mim?" Billy asked his mother the minute he got home.

He could smell ham baking. It crackled and sizzled in the oven as his mother placed sweet potatoes on the rack next to the roasting pan. Marjorie sat at the kitchen table with her speller. Billy didn't see Mim.

"She just got in," Mrs. Cole told him. She used a towel to close the oven door, then nodded toward the stairs that rose to the attic. "Supper is going to be late tonight," she added. "Your father won't be back from the tunnel for another hour. Would you tell Mim when you go up?"

Billy nodded. He was itching to talk to Mim—but not about supper.

In a flash he hung his scarf and jacket on the rack in the parlor. Sure enough, Mim's jacket was there. Billy pawed through the jumble of coats and hats, looking for her scarf.

"Not here," he murmured.

He frowned, fingering the bit of red wool in his pocket. Then he hurried back through the kitchen and pounded upstairs to the attic.

Mim lay on his bed, writing in her diary. She was scribbling so fast and furiously that she didn't notice Billy at first.

"Where's your scarf?" he demanded.

Mim snapped her diary shut and jumped to her feet. "I—um…"

"I know you were at that cave," Billy said quickly. He pulled the bit of red yarn from his pocket and held it up. "Finn and I found this. And some fishing wire. Why'd you steal my new fishing rod, Mim?" The words tumbled from his mouth like water over the falls at Crystal Lake. But before Mim could answer, a hushed voice spoke up behind Billy.

"Quit bugging her!"

He spun around to see Dannie climbing the attic stairs. Finn was right behind her. Dannie glanced back toward the kitchen, then lowered her voice even more.

"Finn told me what you two found," she went on.

"And that you still think Mim is some kind of low-down thief. Well, she's *not!*"

Finn and Billy looked at each other. "Okay, then why'd she pretend to hurt her ankle?" Finn asked. "And why did she take Billy's fishing rod?"

"And why'd she go sneaking up the mountain and trick me into getting stuck on that island?" Billy added.

Mim backed away from them without answering. She sat on a corner of Billy's bed, twisting the blanket in her fingers.

"Because she's trying to help a hurt animal!" Dannie burst out angrily. "You two are going to ruin everything if you don't quit pestering her!"

Billy blinked. For a moment, all he could do was stare at Mim. "You're helping an *animal?*" he asked.

At last she looked up. Her eyes darted nervously from Billy to Finn to Dannie. "Yes," she said quietly.

"Mim told me all about it while we were helping Miss Wrigley today," Dannie explained.

"So *you* made the fire we saw?"

"And what about those creepy pictures on the rocks?" Billy asked. "Did you draw those?"

Mim didn't answer. She looked away. "The...animal has to stay warm. It has to eat—and I can help. It...it needs me!" she said.

"But Mim, stealing things is wrong," said Billy.

Mim looked alarmed. "I didn't steal any money or binoculars or food," she insisted. "Or Mr. Lockhart's coat, either."

Billy noticed she didn't say anything about his fishing rod. "I saw a coat in the cave," he said. "It didn't just get there by itself," he said.

"What about that strange man Alice Ann saw?" Finn added. "Did you see anyone like that, Mim?"

Dannie rolled her eyes. "You know how dramatic Alice Ann is. She probably imagined it. If there was a stranger there, someone else would have seen him, too."

Mim stayed on the edge of Billy's bed, biting her lip. "I'm not doing anything bad. Really. You have to believe me!" she said.

Billy wanted to believe Mim. It would be just like his cousin to help a creature in need. He tried to sort through the questions that swirled inside his head. "Then why'd you make such a big secret of this animal, Mim?" he asked.

"It's sick. Real sick. It's scared of people. I was afraid it might die if it was bothered too much! That's why I moved it away from that cave you found," she explained. She looked at Billy with wide, begging eyes. "You have to trust me. Promise you won't tell anyone! Not even Aunt Ruth and Uncle James."

Billy took a deep breath. "Well...okay," he agreed. "I won't say anything."

"See? Didn't I tell you they would understand?" Dannie said. She turned to Mim with a bright smile.

"Thanks," Mim said. But Billy saw that her eyes were still clouded with worry. Every time he looked at her, she glanced away. She seemed more uncomfortable than ever, and Billy had to wonder why.

There was something else that bothered him, too.

If Mim wasn't the thief, then who was?

* * *

Billy breathed in the cold, pine-scented air as he and Finn headed toward the main part of camp. He was glad Finn had suggested getting some sweets from the cookhouse. After all, his supper wouldn't be ready for a while yet. And the cold evening air helped to clear his mind.

Mim and Dannie had stayed behind to talk about Mim's hurt creature. That was fine with Billy.

"I know we said we wouldn't talk to anyone else about what Mim's doing," he said, breaking the silence. "But we can still talk to each other, right?"

Finn nodded. "Sure," he said.

Billy reached into his pocket and felt the list he and

Mim had started. He couldn't read it in the darkness, but he had memorized every word.

"Mim swears she didn't have anything to do with the stuff that was taken from the family cabins," he said.

"There's still Eddie. He was smoking that cigarette," Finn pointed out.

"Yeah. But why would he take all that food? Or binoculars from Mr. Riley?" Billy wondered out loud. "And how did that coat get into the cave?"

He shivered, stuffing the paper back into his jacket pocket. "I just can't shake the feeling that there's still something Mim's not telling us."

They crossed the river on the footbridge, then followed the road that curved around the main part of camp. The lodge was just ahead. Beyond it were the hospital, cookhouse, and recreation hall. As the cookhouse came into view, Billy saw the back door push open.

"Looks like Eddie came to get some cookies, too," he said to Finn.

The older boy paused on the platform outside the cookhouse. In his hand was a bulging paper sack. *Nothing unusual about that,* Billy thought. Still, he was surprised to see that Eddie didn't follow the walkway toward the road. Instead, he jumped to the ground.

Tucking the paper sack under his arm, he darted into the trees.

"How come he's sneaking through the woods?" Finn whispered. It was almost dark, but Billy could see the scowl on his friend's face.

"There's only one way to find out," Billy said. "Let's follow him!"

In a flash, he and Finn reached the spot where Eddie had disappeared among the trees. The forest was a dark tangle of shadows, but the boys kept going.

The sounds of scuttling creatures made Billy nervous. He made himself listen for the louder sounds of Eddie pushing past the evergreen branches ahead of them.

"This way," he whispered.

Eddie was heading north of the family cabins. At least, that was what Billy guessed. In the darkness, it was hard to tell for sure.

Soon he heard the rushing water of the Tye River. Moonlight filtered through the trees and made shimmering highlights on the water.

Finn pointed to a series of rocks that jutted out of the water. "Eddie's already crossed the river!" he said.

Billy jumped from rock to rock and climbed the bank on the far side of the water. They were near the schoolhouse, he realized. This time of evening, the school was usually closed up tight.

Not tonight.

When Billy and Finn climbed up the bank, they were surprised to see electric lights shining brightly in the schoolhouse windows.

"Jeepers!" Billy said. "What's Eddie doing here now?"

Finn shrugged. "Dunno," he said.

He and Billy crouched on the bank as Eddie jogged up the steps to the schoolhouse. The older boy checked left and right. Then he pulled open the door and disappeared inside.

"Come on!" Billy whispered.

He and Finn ran to the school. Billy yanked open the door and raced inside. Eddie was still in the coatroom. He whirled around, startled.

"What the…?"

Billy charged over to the older boy and grabbed him by the arm. "We've got you this time, Eddie. Now, tell us what you're up to!"

Chapter Eleven

UNANSWERED QUESTIONS

Eddie yanked his arm free of Billy's grasp. "What do you think you're doing? You little sneaks *followed* me!" he sputtered.

His face burned with anger, but Billy and Finn didn't back down.

"You're the sneak!" Finn shot back. "You keep going off and won't tell anyone why. Well, you'd better tell us now!"

"*Ahem!*" a deep voice spoke up behind them. "Is there a problem, boys?"

Billy and Finn whirled around. "Mr. Farnam!" they both said at once.

Their teacher stood with his arms crossed in front of his chest. Instead of his shirt, vest, and long pants, he wore a loose-fitting athletic costume with a sleeveless wool top.

"Aren't you cold?" Billy asked. He couldn't help it.

The coal stove hadn't been lit. Billy's breath made white puffs as he spoke. Mr. Farnam jumped lightly up and down, rubbing his arms.

"I'll warm up just fine as soon as Eddie and I start our wrestling exercises," he said.

"Mr. Farnam!" Eddie burst out. He scowled at the teacher. "You promised you wouldn't tell!"

"Well, we can't have folks in camp thinking you're a thief, Eddie," said Mr. Farnam. He turned his gaze to Billy and Finn. "Isn't that why you boys followed him here? Because you're afraid he's got something to do with the things that were stolen?" he asked.

"That's right, sir," Finn said, nodding.

Mr. Farnam chuckled. "All Eddie is doing is training for next week's junior wrestling match in Skykomish," he said. Stepping over to his desk, he pointed to a hand-bill tacked up beneath the photograph of President Coolidge. Billy saw a drawing of a young wrestler on it.

"I still remember a few tricks from my high school wrestling days," Mr. Farnam explained. "So I'm helping Eddie get in top form."

Eddie stared moodily at the rough-cut floorboards. He wasn't the kind of boy who ever admitted he needed help. Not in public, anyhow.

"Is that why you weren't at the fishing contest and fish fry?" Billy asked. "You were *wrestling?*"

Eddie nodded. "Not that it's any of your beeswax," he said gruffly.

"But…what about that cigarette we saw you smoking?" Finn wanted to know.

"Cigarette?" Mr. Farnam frowned at Eddie.

"We found an Old Gold cigarette behind Alice Ann's cabin on Saturday," Finn explained. "This morning Eddie and Jim had one just like it up on Lookout Rock."

Mr. Farnam turned his concerned gaze to Eddie. "Is this true?" he asked.

Eddie rolled his eyes toward the ceiling. "I wouldn't go near that snooty Alice Ann's cabin for anything. All I did was sneak one cigarette—this morning," he said. He shot Billy a smug look and added, "You want to know where I got it? Maybe you should ask your cousin."

Billy blinked at Eddie. "Mim? What would *she* know about it?" he asked.

"Ask her, not me," Eddie said, shrugging. He nodded toward the door. "Now, beat it. And don't tell anyone Mr. Farnam is helping me."

"Wait! What could *Mim* know about cigarettes?"

Billy asked. He tried to twist around Eddie. But Eddie started pushing him and Finn out the door.

"I'm afraid Eddie's told you all he can," Mr. Farnam said. "He and I have work to do."

"Do you think Mim really has something to do with those cigarettes?" Finn asked Billy when the two of them were outside the schoolhouse. "I mean, how could cigarettes cure some sick creature?"

"I don't know," Billy admitted. "But you can bet I'm going to ask Mim the first chance I get."

* * *

Supper was on the table when Billy got home. He didn't have a chance to talk to Mim until after the dishes were washed. *Sam 'n Henry,* their favorite show, was on the radio. Billy wasn't surprised when Dannie appeared at the door. Her family didn't have a radio. She, Mim, and Billy all flopped down on the rug close to the Coles' set.

Ordinarily Billy loved hearing the hardships and adventures of the two country bumpkins trying to get along in the big city of Chicago. But tonight he couldn't seem to pay attention to Sam and Henry's run-in with a scheming racetrack gambler.

"Think Philip is back in Chicago yet?" Dannie said, turning to look at Billy. "I sure hope he keeps his promise."

With so much going on, Billy had almost forgotten about the promise Philip had made before leaving Scenic.

"What promise?" Mim asked. She raised an eyebrow at Billy and Dannie.

Billy shrugged. "We can have secrets, too, you know," he said.

Mim clamped her mouth shut. Suddenly Billy couldn't wait a second longer to talk to her. He glanced into the kitchen. His parents were still talking at the table. Scooting closer to Mim, he whispered, "Have you been messing with Old Gold cigarettes? Eddie says you have."

Mim's eyes flashed.

"Haven't we been through this already?" said Dannie. "Mim didn't take anything!"

"I'm not doing anything bad," Mim insisted. Wrapping her arms around her legs, she rested her chin on her knees. "You have to believe me, Billy."

Billy frowned at her. "What about the cigarettes?" he asked again.

"You promised not to ask questions," Mim

reminded him. "You're just going to have to trust me, Billy."

She'd said the same thing earlier. But Billy couldn't ignore the feeling that prickled him like the thorny rose vines near Crystal Lake.

Something was very wrong.

Chapter Twelve
STORM WATCH

The next morning the sky outside Billy's window was bleak and gray. A blanket of clouds pressed down on the mountain. It matched the heaviness Billy felt every time he looked at Mim.

"We'll see snow before the day's out," his mother predicted. "Your father's already at the tunnel putting extra crews on. They'll need to keep the tracks clear and the machines running if they're to stay on schedule."

Mim barely seemed to listen. She poked at the pancakes Billy's mother had placed in front of her. "Don't you think the storm might hold off?" she asked. "I might go for a walk up the mountain after school."

Billy had a feeling Mim planned to do more than just walk. She probably wanted to visit the creature she was taking care of.

"Can I go too?" Marjorie asked.

"I should say not!" Mrs. Cole answered. She took the pitcher from Marjorie, who had poured a lake of syrup on her pancakes. "You know how unpredictable these winter storms can be. You children are not to leave camp today. If there's snow, you can play here by the cabins."

"Yes, Aunt Ruth," Mim said.

But Billy saw the worried lines that dug into her forehead. They didn't leave her face all day. Every time Billy caught sight of her at school, Mim was scanning the sky with that same concerned expression.

Snowflakes began to fall, thick and fast, a half hour before the afternoon bell. By the time Mr. Farnam dismissed the students, two inches of fluffy snow covered the school yard. Kids whooped and hollered as they grabbed their coats and hats and ran outside.

"Mim," Billy said, catching up to her in the coatroom. "You're not going up the mountain, are you?" he asked.

Mim pulled on her jacket without answering. Billy didn't like the determined gleam he saw in her eyes. "You promised Mother you wouldn't," he reminded her. "It's too dangerous!"

"Billy? Could you come here a moment?" Mr.

Farnam called from his classroom. "I have something I'd like you to take to your father."

Billy stifled a groan. "Be right there, Mr. Farnam," he said.

He looked away from Mim for just a second. When he turned back, she was darting out the door into a haze of snow.

"Mim, wait!" he said.

The schoolhouse door banged shut behind her.

With a sigh Billy walked over to his teacher's desk. Mr. Farnam held up two shiny, brand-new wooden fishing lures. They had been carved and painted to look like minnows. One was yellow and red. The other was silver and black.

"I promised your dad I'd carve these plugs for him," Mr. Farnam said. He held the lures carefully, keeping his fingers away from the hooks that dangled from the wood. "He said he wanted to send them to Mr. Mackey. Would you take them to his office for me?"

"Sure, Mr. Farnam," said Billy. What else could he say?

He waited while his teacher laid the lures in a small cardboard box and wrapped the box in paper. When Billy ran outside a few minutes later, snowballs were flying in every direction. Dannie and Finn darted about with the other kids, scooping snow and dodging balls.

Mim was nowhere in sight.

"Where's Mim? Did you see her leave?" Billy called to Dannie and Finn.

They didn't seem to hear him. Dannie gave a cry as a snowball hit her red cheek. "I'll get you!" she shouted at Wes. Finn was busy pelting Jim Walsh with snow. With so much snow flying, they probably hadn't noticed where Mim had gone.

Besides, Billy had a delivery to make before he could look for Mim.

"Don't go anywhere!" he yelled to his friends. "I'll be right back!"

* * *

"Thanks, son," Mr. Cole said. Sitting at his desk, he unwrapped the box Billy had handed him. He lifted the lid and inspected the lures, then smiled. "Perfect. I'll send these out to Mr. Mackey in tomorrow's mail. They'll make a fine souvenir of his time in Scenic. Put the box over there, would you?"

Billy's father gestured to a small table overflowing with papers and old clothes. Billy stared at the faded coveralls, old shoes, and flannel shirts. He hesitated to push them aside to make room.

"Never mind about those things," Mr. Cole said. "I've been hanging on to them for a fella who got fired. That hothead Judd Bailey stormed out of camp as mad as all get out. Made all kinds of crazy threats. But he might come back for his things once he cools down."

"Judd?" Billy recalled the dark-haired man he'd seen with his father at the lodge just after Mim had arrived in Scenic. "The one you were talking to before the fishing contest?"

"That's right. After what he did, we couldn't keep him on any longer," Mr. Cole said. "Fool went and lit a cigarette inside the tunnel while the men were setting dynamite charges."

"Jeepers!" Billy exclaimed.

"We're lucky the foreman got it out before anything bad happened," Billy's father went on. "Every man on his crew might have been killed."

Rising to his feet, Mr. Cole took his coat and hat from the rack behind his desk. "I'd better see how the men are coping with this storm," he said as he buttoned his coat over his vest. "Tell your mother not to wait supper for me."

And then he was gone.

Billy was about to follow when a paper caught his eyes. It lay half-crumpled next to Judd's coveralls. The letter was from a bank—some kind of notice about money Judd owed on a loan. But it wasn't the words that caught Billy's eye.

Scrawled across the page were strange hangman drawings—just like the ones Billy and Finn had found outside the cave near Crystal Lake!

Chapter Thirteen
BIG TROUBLE

Oh no!" Billy gasped.

All of a sudden he felt as if he couldn't get enough air.

Judd Bailey was the man in the cave, Billy realized. *He must be the man Alice Ann saw!*

Troubling thoughts raced through his mind so fast he could hardly keep them straight.

His father had said that Judd had stormed from camp in an angry huff. Billy was willing to bet Judd had stolen Mr. Lockhart's coat and those other things from the family cabins before climbing up the mountainside. He had to be the thief.

But why would he hole up in a cave? Billy wondered. Surely there was someplace else he could go.

Billy shivered, remembering what his father had said about Judd making threats. He had no idea what kind of threats the man might have made. But it was bad enough that Judd had been lurking in the woods so close to camp.

The more Billy thought about it, the more worried he felt. Mim had admitted that she'd gone to the cave. Had Judd seen her? Had she perhaps spoken to him while caring for her hurt animal?

What if he was up on the mountain right now—and so was Mim?

"I've got to find her," Billy said out loud.

He turned on his heel and ran from his father's office. Snow was still falling thick and fast. It wasn't until Billy put his hands in his jacket pockets that he realized he was still holding the bank notice with the hangman drawings on it. Crumpling it into a ball, he left it in his pocket and hurried home.

"Mim!" he called as he burst through the door.

There was no answer.

"Mother? Marjorie?" Billy called.

His mother and sister weren't home, either. Billy stomped his boot in frustration, leaving a puddle of melted snow on the floor. Biting his lip, he glanced out through the parlor window. He still saw no sign of

Mim. But he did see two red, snowy, and very familiar faces.

"Finn! Dannie!" he cried, shoving the cabin door open again. "Mim's in trouble!"

* * *

"Jeepers!" Finn stared at the hangman drawings on the crumpled notice Billy held out. "This Judd Bailey fellow *must* be the one who was in the cave!"

"And the one who stole all that stuff," Dannie added.

Billy's story of what he'd learned spilled out as his friends pulled off their hats, jackets, scarves, and boots. Dannie frowned as she shook the snow from her wet things and hung them on the rack. She and Finn followed Billy through the kitchen and up the steps to the attic.

"Do you think Mim's got something to do with that man? That she's up on the mountain *now?*" Dannie asked. Right away she shook her head. "No. She's got better sense than that."

"Then where is she?" Finn asked. "She didn't stay in the school yard to play. And she sure isn't here."

Billy glanced around the attic. His gaze lingered on his bed. Mim's diary lay on top of it.

"No," said Dannie firmly. She shook her head. "That's private!"

"But we need to find Mim. Maybe she wrote down where she's hiding her hurt animal!" Billy argued. "If we can find the creature, I bet we'll find Mim, too."

He was already striding toward the bed. Dannie scowled when he reached for Mim's diary. But she came with Finn to sit next to him. He opened the diary.

"We won't read all of it," Billy promised. "Just what she's written since she got to Scenic."

Mim's messy handwriting filled three-quarters of the diary. Billy flipped through the pages until he came to the last few entries. "Here's something about the fishing contest," he said.

He held out the diary so that Finn and Dannie could see it, too:

Saturday, November 6

Dear Diary,
Today was full of firsts. The first time I beat Billy at mar -
bles. The first time I caught more fish than him. The first time
I ever ran a projector. The first time I ever won five dollars. Five
whole dollars! Yippee!

There was a little break, and then Mim had added something in smaller, unsteady handwriting:

Today was the first time I ever hurt Billy's feelings, too.

"We don't have to read this," Billy said quickly. He flipped ahead and skimmed the page. "This next part is just wondering about who stole the things from camp," he said.

"What about this?" Finn jabbed at the next page with his finger. "She wrote it on Monday afternoon after Mr. Farnam took us up the mountain for school."

"Right *after* she pretended to hurt her ankle! That's when she started acting funny," Billy added. He began reading:

Dear Diary,
I have a secret. A secret so big it'll make me burst if I don't write about it. A secret so big I had to lie to everyone at school and even to Billy....

Billy gulped and glanced at Dannie. She frowned as her eyes moved down the page. Billy quickly read on:

I wouldn't have done it, but someone needs my help. He's

awfully sick, and he says taking a mountain cure is his only hope. It's bad for him to be around folks. He says it might even kill him! That's why I had to lie. He said I can come back because I make him feel better. I think I will give him my scarf. He needs it more than I do....

"Criminy!" Finn said, looking up from the page. "Mim isn't helping a hurt animal. She's helping a person—that fellow your dad fired, Billy!"

Dannie's face went white. "She lied to me," she said, still staring down at Mim's words. "She lied to all of us."

Billy understood why Dannie was upset. He was upset, too. But Mim's lying wasn't what worried him the most.

"Dad didn't say anything about Judd Bailey being sick. What if Mr. Bailey made up that story to trick Mim?" he said. "What if she's up on the mountain with him right now?"

"If she is," said Finn slowly, "then she could be in big trouble."

CHAPTER FOURTEEN

INTO THE BLIZZARD

"We've got to warn Mim," said Dannie. "Right now. Before the storm gets even worse!"

She jumped up from Billy's bed and headed for the kitchen. Billy and Finn pounded down the stairs behind her.

"Mother and Marjorie can't have gone far," Billy said. "We can leave a note telling Mother where we've gone."

"But we don't know where we're going," Finn pointed out. "We don't even know where Mim is!"

Billy was already pulling on his jacket and boots. "We'll follow her tracks. Anyone who comes after us can follow *our* tracks," he said.

Billy wasn't sure they would be able to find Mim's tracks. Falling snow had probably covered them by now. But he knew they had to try.

"Let's go!" he said.

The clearing next to the cabins was filled with boys and girls throwing snowballs and digging in the snow. Voices called out to Billy, Finn, and Dannie, but they ignored the shouts as they hurried along the path to the schoolhouse.

Snow fell in a haze so thick it was hard to see. Fluffy powder already lay half a foot thick on the ground. The mountain above the schoolhouse looked as if a white blanket had been draped over it. The path up to Lookout Rock was a slippery mess. Billy was wet and breathless by the time he and his friends finally climbed onto the big granite ledge.

Snow covered the rock. But Billy grew hopeful when he saw a line of marks in the snow. "Mim went that way!" he said, pointing.

"Up the old Indian path," Finn added. He squinted ahead. There was snow on his hat, scarf, and jacket—even on his eyelashes.

He, Billy, and Dannie followed the dimpled path, pushing through the snow with their boots. Billy had never seen the forest so quiet and still. Snow muffled all sound. He glimpsed deer and snowshoe hares in the distance, but they seemed to move in absolute silence. Billy was quiet, too. He put all his energy into following Mim's faint footprints.

Just before Crystal Lake, he stopped. The snow on the trail ahead, toward the lake, was undisturbed. Mim's footprints veered left, away from the trail.

"Looks like she went north," Dannie said, stopping next to him.

"Right where we found that cave," Finn said. He sprinted off the path, heading into the forest.

Billy's hands and feet felt numb, but a fresh burst of energy helped to warm him. He and Dannie hurried through the snow after Finn. Before long they caught sight of the slanted rocks that framed the cave Billy and Finn had found.

Finn shot a surprised glance over his shoulder. Billy saw why. Mim's footprints continued *past* the cave.

"Judd Bailey must have found another place to hole up," Billy said. Shivering, he plodded on. He wasn't sure how far they'd gone when he heard Dannie gasp.

"Over there!" she whispered.

Looking ahead, Billy saw a ragged, dark hole in the snow-covered hillside. It was *another* cave, he realized. And Mim's footprints led straight to it.

"We found her!" Billy leaped past Finn. "Mim!" he shouted.

A trail of smoke rose from the cave into the snowy air. A big boulder blocked most of the cave's entrance. Squeezing past, Billy spotted Mim. She was crouched next to a fire close to the opening. She glanced up from the trout she was roasting over the fire on a stick. Billy's brand-new fishing rod lay near the fire on the rock floor of the cave.

"Billy!" Mim jumped up, dropping the fish to the ground. "What are you doing? You'll ruin everything!"

Her eyes darted toward the shadowy depths of the cave behind her. As Billy ducked inside, he saw a man lying on the ground. A dirty coat was spread over him like a blanket. The man pushed himself up on one elbow. Billy saw dark hair and eyes full of suspicion. It made Billy mad to see Mim's red scarf, now matted with dirt, wrapped around the man's neck.

"We know all about Judd Bailey," Finn said as he and Dannie came into the cave, too.

"You lied to us, Mim," Dannie added.

Mim's eyes clouded over. "I had to! Mr. Bailey's taking a mountain cure. He needs to be alone or it won't work—"

"We don't believe that," Billy said, facing the man. "You're not sick at all, Mr. Bailey. You're just mad 'cause my dad fired you! That's why you stole all those things from camp."

The glow from the fire shimmered on something small and black on the floor next to Judd. Billy spotted the lenses of a pair of binoculars.

"I thought someone was watching me," Billy went on. "When I went off into the woods after the fishing contest. It was you, wasn't it?"

Judd Bailey didn't answer. He just sat there, rubbing his chin and staring at Billy. "So you're Mr. Cole's boy, eh?" he murmured.

"Mr. Bailey's not bad. He had to borrow things to stay alive!" Mim insisted. "Tell them, Mr. Bailey. Tell them what you told me. That you might die without the peace and quiet of the mountain air."

Billy knew some folks believed in the healing powers of mountain air. But Judd Bailey looked more sneaky than sick. His sharp eyes were like a weasel's, shifting all over without settling in one place.

"He made threats, Mim," Billy told his cousin. "Against Dad. Against everyone in camp. Ever since he left he's been up here stewing over how to get revenge!"

"On Uncle James?" Mim shook her head furiously back and forth. "N—no. That can't be. Mr. Bailey wouldn't do that."

The scruffy man barely seemed to listen. While everyone else talked, he unwound Mim's scarf from his neck. He ran a finger over the name that Billy's mother had stitched next to the fringe in black. "Miriam Cole," he murmured, chuckling. "This is too good...."

Mim frowned. "Mr. Bailey? What are you…"

All at once Judd Bailey leaped to his feet. He lunged toward Mim, grabbing her roughly by the shoulders.

Mim screamed.

"Let her go!" Dannie shouted. But Billy could see she was afraid to move. She and Finn stood stock still right next to Billy.

"W—why are you hurting me?" Mim squeaked out.

"I'm afraid your friends are right, Mim," Bailey said. "I did trick you."

Mim gulped. Billy saw her eyes fill with terror.

"You see, you caught me by surprise when you and your little classmates were playing," Judd went on. "I couldn't have you telling anyone I was here. Then I'd never have the chance to get back at Mr. Cole for what he did to me. So I made up a story."

"You deserved to be fired!" Dannie said. "You could have killed everyone inside the tunnel!"

She has every right to be mad, Billy thought. Dannie's own father worked on one of the crews that set the dynamite charges.

If her words bothered Judd Bailey, he didn't show it.

"Of course, it took me a while to come up with a plan," he went on. "But Mim here was nice enough to help keep me comfortable in the meantime."

A box of cigarettes stuck out of Judd Bailey's pocket.

Finn frowned when he saw them. "Did he make you get those, Mim?" Finn asked.

She nodded miserably. "I bought them at the store yesterday morning. I hid them next to Lookout Rock, but I guess Eddie found the box and took one."

Billy didn't like the cold, calculating way Judd Bailey was watching him and Mim. "What are you going to do now, Mr. Bailey?" he asked.

"Oh, you'll see," the man said, smiling.

Keeping a firm hold on Mim, he backed toward the cave entrance. All but a narrow slit was blocked by the boulder Billy had squeezed past to get in. When the man was right next to the opening, he shoved Mim hard. She flew toward the fire.

"Mim!" Billy leaped forward, grabbing her. Both of them tumbled toward the flames. At the last second, Finn and Dannie yanked them to the side. Billy and Mim thudded to the rock floor next to the fire.

Billy quickly rose to his elbows and twisted around—just in time to see the boulder grind shut over the cave entrance. A creepy laugh came from right outside.

"Want to know how I'll get revenge?" Judd Bailey called. He laughed again—a low cackle that chilled Billy to the bone. "By making sure Mr. James Cole never sees his son, or his niece, again."

CHAPTER FIFTEEN

TRAPPED!

Billy felt a cold knot of fear in the pit of his stomach. It twisted and grew as he stared at the damp, dark rock walls of the cave.

"We're trapped!" he said.

His friends' faces were pale in the firelight. Mim stared at him with a shocked, half-dazed expression. "You mean Mr. Bailey's just going to leave us here to...die?" she whispered.

"He can't do that!" Dannie ran to the boulder and pushed against it. "Hey! Let us out!" she yelled.

Billy, Finn, and Mim ran to join her. Digging in with their boots, they heaved and shoved against the rough stone.

The boulder didn't budge.

"Mr. Bailey!" Finn shouted.

They heard grunting and the scraping noise of something being dragged through the snow. Billy pressed his face close to a ragged sliver of light between the boulder and the cave wall.

"He's wedged a log in next to the rock," Billy said. "We'll never move it now!"

"That's right," Judd Bailey's voice came again from outside the cave. "With this storm, it'll be days before anyone can get up here to look for you. Maybe longer. Who knows? They might never find this cave at all."

"But...but I helped you, Mr. Bailey!" Mim cried out. Billy saw tears trickle down her cheeks. "You can't just leave us here!"

"Oh, no?"

Judd Bailey didn't say anything more. Billy peered through the narrow crack next to the boulder. The man was walking away from the cave into a blinding swirl of snow.

"He's gone," Billy said, sighing.

He slid to sit on the cave floor, his back against the boulder. For a long moment, the only sound inside the cave was the crackling of the fire. The air grew smokier. It stung Billy's lungs, and he started to cough.

"This is all my fault," Mim said. She stared into the smoky depth of the cave—then blinked. "Hey—look at the smoke!"

At first Billy didn't know what she was making such a big deal about. The choking smoke was everywhere. But then he saw the cloud twist and rise toward the roof of the cave. "It's getting sucked out of the cave!" he said excitedly. "There must be a hole!"

"Maybe there's a way out of here after all!" Finn ran to the corner of the cave and looked up. "There *is* a hole. Quick, Billy, give me your fishing rod. Maybe we can dig it out more!"

The hole was tiny—just an inch or so across. But dirt and rocks fell away when Finn poked at it with Billy's fishing rod. Billy, Mim, and Dannie took turns propping each other up so they could dig with their hands, too. Before long the hole was big enough for Mim to squeeze through. Snowflakes fell on Billy as he climbed on Finn's shoulders and pulled himself up after her, into the bright, snowy daylight.

They were on the slope just above the boulder that blocked the cave entrance, Billy realized. He frowned at the large log that was wedged next to the rock.

"We need to get help," he said.

"But Mr. Bailey will get away!" Mim bit her lip, staring at the trail the man had left in the snow. "We have to stop him."

"You guys go!" Finn called from inside the cave. "Dannie and I'll get help as soon as we get out."

Mim was already pushing through the snow. Billy recognized the determined gleam in her eyes. He knew there was no way to talk her out of going after Judd Bailey. "Wait up!" he called.

The storm was even worse now. Snow lay more than knee deep on the ground and was still falling fast. Biting winds whipped the flakes into a frenzy.

Billy and Mim could hardly see more than a foot in front of them. Squinting, they somehow managed to follow in Judd Bailey's tracks. Billy had no idea where they were—or where they were going. Every breath of ice-cold air made his lungs ache. But he and Mim pushed themselves harder and harder.

"There!" Mim said. She stopped, gasping for air, next to the snow-covered branches of a fallen fir tree.

Billy peered into the blinding swirl of snow. They were at the top of a steep hillside, he saw. He had to blink a few times before he could make out the figure of a man moving down the slope.

"Come on!" Mim started down the hillside, but Billy grabbed her jacket.

"Wait! I've got an idea," Billy said. "If Mr. Bailey can use trees, so can we!"

He pushed at the dead, snow-covered fir tree that lay next to them. It rolled half over, to the edge of the steep hillside. Mim looked at the tree, then stared down the hillside.

"It'll knock him right down! It's a clear path—if we go fast. Let's go!" she said.

Billy could barely hear her over the howling wind. He nodded, and they both shoved at the tree. Dried branches scraped Billy's face, but he didn't care. They kept on pushing until the tree toppled over the edge of the hillside. It rolled over and over, picking up speed.

Judd Bailey never even saw it coming. The tree smacked into him and Billy saw the man fly forward in a shower of snow.

"I think the tree's on top of him," Billy said, peering down the hillside.

He and Mim slipped and slid down the steep, snowy slope. As they got closer, Billy saw the man's legs sticking out from beneath the tree. A low groan sounded from underneath the prickly branches.

"My leg...I'm hurt," Judd Bailey moaned. He scowled through the branches at Billy and Mim. "How did you...?"

"We've got a few tricks of our own, Mr. Bailey," Mim told him.

"Help is on the way," Billy added. "And when it gets here, you're going to jail."

* * *

"Time to go, Mim!" Aunt Delia called from the steps of Billy's cabin. "Your father and I want to get back to Berne before suppertime."

Sunshine sparkled down from the cloudless sky. Three days had passed since the storm. It had taken that long to clear the roads and tracks of the four feet of snow that had fallen. When Mim's parents drove into camp on Saturday morning, snow was piled as high as the eaves of the cabins in some spots.

"Can't I play longer?" Mim called back. She patted down the walls of a snow fort that she and Dannie were building in the clearing. Billy and Finn were hard at work on their own fort, next to the river.

"I think you've had enough adventure for one trip, Miriam Cole," Aunt Delia said.

That's for sure, thought Billy. But everything had turned out all right in the end. Judd Bailey was behind bars in the Skykomish jail. And Billy, Mim, Dannie, and Finn had made it back to camp safe and sound.

"Sorry for all the trouble I caused," Mim said as she brushed the snow from her mittens. "I guess I should have known not to trust a stranger who wanted me to keep secrets from my own family."

She smiled at Billy. "I guess I have a few things to learn from you yet," she added.

Billy was climbing the steps to his cabin when he saw his father and Uncle Herb. They were making their way across the footbridge that crossed to the family cabins from the main camp. Billy's father waved an envelope in the air. "Kids! There's a letter for you! From Philip!"

Billy saw the excited looks that flashed between Finn and Dannie. They came flying through the snow toward Billy's cabin. "Let's see!" Dannie said. "Do you think he remembered his promise?"

"What promise?" Mim asked.

Billy didn't answer right away. Taking the envelope from his father, he ripped it open. Inside was a glossy photograph of two men dressed to look like country bumpkins.

"It's Sam and Henry!" Aunt Delia said in surprise. "How ever did you get that, Billy?"

"From Philip," Billy answered. "He promised to send it to me. You see, he's met the real Sam 'n Henry—the men who play the parts on the radio, that is."

"Look! He even got them to sign the photograph," Dannie added.

She pointed to the words scrawled across the bottom of the photograph: *For Billy Cole, with our warmest regards.*

It was signed *Charles "Henry Johnson" Correll and Freeman "Sam Smith" Gosden.*

"Gee whiz! You sure are lucky," Mim said.

Before Billy could answer, a snowball hit him square on the back of the head. He turned to see Alice Ann smirking at him.

"Take that, Billy Cole!" she shouted.

By now Janet, Lucy, and some of the other girls had joined Alice Ann. Finn threw a snowball at them, then called to Billy. "It's boys against girls!"

Billy shoved his photograph of Sam 'n Henry into Aunt Delia's hands. Then he reached down to scoop up some snow.

But just as he did, another snowball hit him on the shoulder.

"Gotcha!" Mim called gleefully.

Billy threw his own snowball back at his cousin. "This is one contest you won't win!" he shouted back.

"We'll see about that," Mim said.

Billy grinned. Everything was back to normal now. He and Mim were friends again.

But there was no way he'd let her beat him *this* time.

Author's Note

I got the idea for the CASCADE MOUNTAIN RAILROAD
MYSTERIES from a surprising place—a calendar! This calendar was made by my uncle, David Conroy, and was all
about the building of
the Cascade Tunnel.
Until I saw it, I hadn't
realized my grand-
father was the general
manager in charge of
building the Cascade
Tunnel. He brought
his family—my Grandma
Conroy, Uncle Dave, and my
mom—to live in Scenic while the
tunnel was being built. Grandpa
Conroy saved lots of photographs,
and my uncle used
some of them in his calendar.

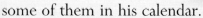
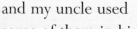

As soon as I saw the picture of children
outside Scenic's two-room schoolhouse (my
uncle is the rascal in the white shirt in the
second row, third from the right), I wanted
to know more. More about the tunnel. More about the
Scenic camp. More about what it was like to be a kid in

Scenic back then. I started asking questions, and the result is THE CASCADE MOUNTAIN RAILROAD MYSTERIES.

THE CASCADE MOUNTAIN RAILROAD MYSTERIES are fictional stories, but I've tried to make the setting as much like the real Scenic as possible. The old lodge, family cabins, cookhouse, and schoolhouse were all part of the real camp. Silent movies were shown in the recreation hall, with one of the ladies playing piano accompaniment. Crystal Lake, the Tye River, and the old Indian trail are also real. Other sites—like Lookout Rock and the cave Billy found—were invented for the story. Also, I must admit that the map of Scenic in this book is entirely made up! After three-quarters of a century, it is difficult to know exactly where everything was, but I have tried to capture the spirit of the place.

Why the Railroad Needed a Tunnel

Before the eight-mile Cascade Tunnel was built, crossing the Cascade Mountains was dangerous—especially in the winter. Avalanches were a constant threat. The Great Northern Railroad tried to protect its trains by building wooden shelters over the tracks called snowsheds. But the snowsheds weren't always enough. In 1910, an avalanche swept two trains off the tracks and 150 feet down into a canyon. 101 people were killed.

A shorter tunnel, just 2.6 miles long, had already been built higher up the mountain. The Great Northern Railroad decided to build a new, longer tunnel lower on the mountainside, where snowslides were less of a danger. When the new Cascade Tunnel was finished in 1929, it was the longest tunnel in the United States. It is still one of the longest tunnels in the world today.

Diagram of Cascade Tunnel route

Feeding a Hungry Camp

Feeding workers in the Scenic camp was an important job. Twenty-four hours a day, seven days a week, men were on shift inside the tunnel. That meant hungry workers needed food day and night. Chef Ronas and his crew of bakers and chefs (there were almost twenty of them!) made sure plenty of good, home-cooked food was always on hand. With hundreds of people to cook for at a time, Chef Ronas had to think big. When one of the ladies asked him for his cake recipe, he began, "Well, you start with six dozen eggs…"

Scenic bakers

It wasn't easy to keep the camp stocked with food. In winter, roads and railways were often blocked by snows. But the men needed milk, bread, meat, and vegetables. Babies

Scenic cookhouse crew

were born in Scenic while their fathers toiled inside the tunnel, and they needed food, too. When trucks and trains couldn't get through, caterpillar tractors pulled five-

Winters were tough in Scenic.

ton trailers filled with provisions through forests, up steep hills, through snowdrifts, and over rough roads to the camp. The Great Northern Railway made sure supplies came through, no matter what.

Native Americans in Scenic

Long before European settlers came to the area we now call Washington State, native tribes lived there. Indian tribes hunted, fished, and gathered berries in the Cascade Mountains.

Skykomish tribe in ceremonial dress

The town of Skykomish, just west of Scenic, was named for one of these tribes, the Skykomish. (The name comes from two Indian words: *skaikh* meaning "inland" and *mish* meaning "people.") The Skykomish Indians were known for being fast on their feet. They lived in the area near Scenic only during the warm weather. The snowy winter months were spent in villages downstream, off the mountains.

The Snowy Cascades

The Cascade Mountains can get plenty of snowfall in the winter. During the 1920s, six feet of snow—or more!—often blanketed the mountains for months at a time. Workers in the Scenic camp prepared for snowy weather by building raised walkways. These walkways were six feet high and ran between the bunkhouses, tunnel entrance, cookhouse, recreation hall, and other main buildings. That way, men could get around camp without having to trudge through snows that were over their

Raised walkways ran between the Scenic camp's bunkhouses.

heads. The children of Scenic weren't so lucky, though. They had to make their way to the schoolhouse each day without the help of the walkways.

In 1926

☐ Many people did not yet understand the dangers of smoking cigarettes. Some men and women thought smoking was a relaxing—and even glamorous—pastime. The most popular brands of cigarettes were Old Gold, Chesterfield, Lucky Strike, Camel, and Clown. Each brand had its own distinctive box.

☐ Videocassettes and DVDs did not yet exist. Silent movies were made on a film called cellulose nitrate, which was wound onto metal reels and threaded onto projectors. As the reels moved, the images were

Running a movie could be hard work!

A movie poster from 1926

projected onto the screen. Each reel held 2000 feet of film and lasted for just twenty minutes. That meant an hour-long movie had to be shown on three separate reels. Cellulose film sometimes snapped, interrupting the movie. And it was flammable. Projector lamps sometimes grew so hot that the film caught fire! It wasn't until the 1950s that the movie industry started using a safer type of film.

◻ Many children liked to play marbles. There were different ways to play, but the most popular was a game called "Ringer." A circle, or ring, was drawn, and the marbles were arranged in an X at the center. Each player used a shooter marble to try to knock marbles from the ring. Whoever had the most marbles at the end was the winner.

Boys playing marbles

About the Author

Anne Capeci has written many mysteries and other books for children, including titles in popular series such as WISHBONE MYSTERIES, MAGIC SCHOOL BUS SCIENCE CHAPTER BOOKS, and MAD SCIENCE. She is also the author of CASCADE MOUNTAIN RAILROAD MYSTERIES BOOK 1: DANGER: DYNAMITE!; BOOK 2: DAREDEVILS; and BOOK 3: GHOST TOWN. Anne lives in Brooklyn, New York, with her husband and two children.